SNOWFLAKES AND SHOTS

A HOLIDAY ROMANCE NOVEL
BOOK 5

AMANDA SIEGRIST

McCord Family Novel

Protecting You

Trust in Love

Deserving You

Always Kind of Love

Finding You

Dare You to Love

Mona & Mason

The Paranormal Chronicles, Volume I

Perfect For You Novel

The Wrong Brother

The Right Time

The Easy Part

The Hard Choice

Psychic Love Novel

Exploding Love

Captured Love

Slaying Love Novel

Won't Let You Go

Doomed Love

Deadly Crazy

Evidence of Sin

Finding Redemption

Obsessed Hope

Short Stories

Paint By Murder

Follow Me, Sweet Darling

Sleighville Novel

Dashing Through the Fear

Here Comes Chaos

The Last Noel

Standalone Novel

The Danger with Love

Conquering Fear Novel

Co-written with Jane Blythe

Drowning in You

Out of the Darkness

Closing In

MERRY CHRISTMAS.

MAY YOUR DAYS AND NIGHTS BE FILLED WITH HOLIDAY CHEER!

1

STU LOOKED UP, pausing in wiping the counter down. A few years ago, he would've internally groaned at the sight of this customer.

But people could change. Sometimes.

Tossing the rag in the small sink near him, he ambled down to the other side of the bar with a friendly smile. One he didn't have to force out. Kind of. It was the holidays, and he usually had to force out a smile during the holidays depending on the person he spoke to. Well, okay, only one person he had to force a smile out for. His father. Best not to think about him, though. It always brought his mood down.

On occasion, he also had to fake a smile for his mom. He never wanted her to feel bad. When it came to holiday festivities, he usually had to pretend like he cared—which he didn't; at least, if it had to do with his father. With Christmas so close, she hounded him about this Christmas thing and that Christmas thing.

He didn't care.

Not if it involved his father.

He wasn't into any Christmas thing if *he* was there. He had no problem with Christmas. He only had a problem with one person in particular who liked to force things on him he didn't want to be involved in. And he loved to do it during the holidays, like it would soften him up or something.

Seriously, though. He didn't want to think about his father at a time like this. So, he wiped his mind clear of any disturbing thoughts and stopped in front of his new customer.

"James. Welcome back to town," Stu said, meaning the sentiment. Surprisingly.

He had to give James credit. He had worked hard to turn his life around. Stopped the drinking, stopped getting in trouble with the law. Stopped being an asshole. He had found love and a new sense on life. That wasn't always easy to do. Although James had given him a hard time—quite a bit—back then, he had apologized for his behavior and Stu wasn't the kind of guy to hold grudges. He had to admit, he was curious why James was here. In his bar. Especially when he didn't drink anymore.

"Good to see you, Stu." James grinned. His eyes trailed to a few bottles behind the counter.

"You ordering something?"

He didn't want to hear the answer to that question. Because then Stu would be forced to make a decision. Serve him alcohol and help him break his sobriety or deny him any drink and help him keep his sobriety.

Well, it wasn't a hard decision to make—he'd say no and help James keep his sobriety—but how would James react? He wasn't in the mood to get into a fight tonight.

James's grin dimmed. "No. Well, yeah, I'll take some water."

Thank goodness for that. Stu nodded and grabbed a glass, popping a few cubes in and then poured water to the top.

"You're probably wondering what I'm doing here." James chuckled. "I'm clean and sober. Haven't had a drop in three years."

"Good for you. You should be proud." Stu leaned back against the counter and matched James's light chuckle. "I am a bit curious why you're here. Where's Erin? How are you guys doing in Florida?"

This was one of the parts Stu loved best about owning and working in a bar—talking to people, getting to know them, letting them share their woes on occasion. Connecting and being real with people. There was nothing better. He had always been a people person. Probably why his father continually tried to suck him into a dream he didn't want to follow.

"Florida is heaven compared to this cold." James laughed as he shook his head. "We're happy there. She's at my sister's right now. They're baking cookies and other shit with Lynn and Emma, and I needed to get out of the house. I didn't know where to go and..." He shrugged. "I saw the place was open and stopped."

That all made sense. A house full of women, chatting girl talk, baking, and no other guys to talk with, Stu would've wanted to leave as well. Except, James didn't have any friends in town. He burned a lot of bridges back in the day when he was drunk all the time. The one guy he always hung out with was a loser of the worst kind. James had cut him out of his life. And who wouldn't? The guy tried to hurt James's sister Theresa.

James glanced around. "Kind of dead for a Monday night."

Besides James, less than ten people were in the bar. Everyone was scattered around. His regulars were playing pool in the corner. A group of locals, Drew, Tom, and Sam, guys in their mid-thirties, not married, no kids, and they enjoyed playing pool. A usual ritual for them every Monday. Stu liked the quiet nights. Monday through Wednesday generally were.

"Yeah, the quiet is nice. Come back this weekend and it'll be rowdier." Not that Stu wanted to tempt James. He already felt like James was tempting fate right now. "Well, maybe not this weekend as it'll be Christmas. Most week-ends are busy."

He honestly didn't want to know how James would react if he changed his mind and asked for a drink that would ruin his sobriety—and Stu told him no. It wasn't his job to stop him from making mistakes. But he was damn proud of James, so he also wanted to make sure he didn't make the wrong mistake.

"There's a lot going on this weekend. Erin's sister Aria is coming here for Christmas and we're going to show her around and stuff." James shrugged again. "Not that Mulberry has much to see, but you know. Show her a good time."

"I hope you all have a great time."

He knew he wouldn't. He always tried for his mother, but it usually didn't work. Christmas always brought bad memories back in full force. Not that they were truly terrible memories, but memories just the same. Memories he didn't care to relive. He always worked to dispel the memories and to have a good excuse when his mother came around badgering him to join them for the holidays. Nope. He wasn't having any of that. So, he worked.

He had three other employees who helped him on the weekends. The closer it got to Christmas, he usually made sure they had off to spend time with their families. Being a small town, the bar didn't get too busy around Christmas. Everyone liked to be at home with their families—well, most everyone. In the past few years, he debated closing the bar on Christmas Eve due to how slow it could get, but there were a few locals who enjoyed coming in. He hated to ruin their holiday routine. He always closed the bar on Christmas Day, which gave him no excuse to use with his mother. He didn't want to be considered a heartless son, so he always showed up to give his mother a present, but he never stayed. He hated the sadness in her eyes every time, but the faster he made the visit, the better it was for everyone involved.

Christmas was one week away.

It couldn't come fast enough and move right on past New Year's.

He decorated the bar for New Year's, but not Christmas. No one ever asked why not. They all knew his uncle never decorated for the holidays, and when the bar was turned over to him, he just kept up the odd tradition.

He didn't play Christmas music either. His playlist varied from country to pop to rock, but never holiday music. Sometimes a rare Christmas song popped up into the playlist. He always had to suffer through it because changing the song would incite questions, and he liked to avoid questions if possible. Because sometimes people couldn't help themselves. They had to ask the questions he wanted to ignore.

"If I had my way, I would whisk Erin away to Terry's cabin and spend Christmas with just the two of us."

"Well, you could always spend a day or two there before or after Christmas. How long you guys in town for?"

"We leave two days after Christmas. I'm not sure we'll be able to sneak away for some alone time. We got in late last night and Erin has been nonstop visiting everyone around town. She missed this place."

Stu couldn't hold in his chuckle. "I'm guessing you don't."

With the bad memories James had, Stu wouldn't blame him.

He had his own bad memories, different from James's but not enough where he wanted to leave the only home he'd ever known. He had too many friends here he'd miss. Plus, he owned a bar. He had roots here.

James cocked his brow in a disbelieving look. "The only thing I miss is my sister." Then he took a sip of water and stood up. "I should get back. It was nice chatting, Stu."

He nodded, surprised how much he agreed. When James wasn't acting like a drunken asshole, he was nice to converse with.

"Have a great visit."

James eyed him funny, probably wondering why he didn't say have a great Christmas or something. But Stu rarely said anything to that effect unless someone initiated it first. Even then, he responded with "you, too."

Hell, he wasn't a complete Grinch. He handed out a few presents to his friends. Joined parties when he was invited— as long as his father wouldn't be in attendance. Which was rare.

He didn't hate the holiday.

He honestly didn't. But he'd gotten so used to pretending he disliked the holiday because of *him* it was natural to keep up the act.

Stu smiled when James finally nodded. Then he turned. Stu couldn't hold in an internal groan this time. A full-blown, annoyed groan escaped when he saw Dusty stop James in his tracks.

"Well, well, look what kind of trash blew in here. Can't believe you let this asshole in here," Dusty said, slightly slurred.

Just. Great.

He was the last person he wanted to deal with on a genuinely nice, peaceful night. And he was already drunk to boot.

"How much have you already had, Dusty?" Stu usually liked to keep the peace with everyone, even a jackass like Dusty. But sometimes, enough was enough.

"A little." Dusty took a step forward. James didn't move. His stance looked rigid. "I'll take a beer. You want a beer, James?"

"I thought you were in prison. For burning down my sister's house," James said, leaning closer. His words came out clipped and harsh.

Shit.

If he didn't do something, these two would break out in a fight, and that's the last thing he wanted to deal with. Bar fights were never fun—or clean.

"Got out a few months ago. Good behavior," Dusty sneered. "My beer, Stu!"

"You can leave, Dusty. I'm not serving you anything when you sound like you've already had enough."

Dusty shoved past James, nudging him hard shoulder to shoulder and slammed his hands on the bar. "I want a damn beer. You can't kick me out for no damn reason."

Stu crossed his arms, praying for patience.

But it was the holidays.

He never had patience during the holidays.

"My bar, my rules. You need to leave."

"Yet, you'll serve this piece of shit," Dusty hollered, throwing a hand in James's direction.

"You're the piece—"

"James, leave this to me, please." Stu cut him off before he could finish a sentence he wholeheartedly agreed with. Dusty *was* a piece of shit.

While James had made mistakes in life, he made amends. He worked hard to turn his life around.

Dusty, on the other hand, since he had been released from prison for arson, still caused problems wherever he went. Not enough to get himself arrested, considering he was on parole and needed to maintain good behavior, but enough to be the Grade A jackass he always was.

"Yeah, James, leave it to Stu. You're nothing but a needle dick coward." Dusty smirked. "How's your sister Theresa? She is one fine piece of ass. I always wanted to tap that." James's jaw clenched, a muscle ticking in his cheek. "Stu asked you to leave. I suggest you do that."

"What you gonna do if I don't?"

"I'll call the cops, Dusty. Just leave so I don't have to do that. You are on parole," Stu replied before James could say anything. He honestly didn't want to see James get into a fight, even though he'd have every right to let loose his anger for the shit Dusty was saying. Stu wanted to kick his ass for saying such things about Theresa—one of the sweetest women in town.

Dusty slammed his fist against the bar again. It took everything in Stu not to jump. "I want a damn beer."

"Yo, man, Stu asked you to leave. Just go," Drew, one of the guys playing pool, said from across the bar.

"No one asked you, asshole," Dusty said right before he

picked up a barstool and threw it in his direction. Then he turned toward James and threw a punch.

All hell broke loose.

Stu vaulted over the counter as James delivered a punch in return.

"Run Rudolph Run" suddenly popped over the speaker as Dusty came at him with a fist. Unlike the song that shouldn't be playing, he wasn't going to run.

This was his bar. His rules.

With the Christmas song blaring in his ears, it fueled his ire.

Dusty wanted a bar fight? He'd give him a bar fight.

CHASITY SIGHED and gripped the side console of the door as Doug flipped on the sirens and headed to the address that came through the radio.

Seriously.

Not a place she wanted to go.

Hafferty's Bar.

Her heart started to pound for two different reasons.

One, because it usually pounded when they had to turn on the ambulance sirens. It meant someone was hurt and she hated knowing she was about to walk into a situation where she needed to help someone. What kind of situation? How bad were they injured? Was it life-threatening? Or minor where they wouldn't need transport to the hospital? So many questions. All unanswered until they arrived to assess the situation. But she loved her job. Loved helping people. But her heart always raced until she arrived to see everything for her own eyes.

The second reason, because she'd have to see him—Stu

Hafferty. The only man to ever capture her pounding heart. The only man to break that same aching heart.

It was a small town—very, very small town. But she did well avoiding him and never having to see him. If her memory served right, the last time she saw him—from a distance, thankfully—was three months ago at the grocery store. She had stepped out of the cereal aisle—because she was no gourmet cook—and he had been leaving the meat counter. They had stared at each other. For a few long seconds. Then he turned his cart around and ventured off into the other direction. It hurt. Like it always did when he ignored her.

But she ignored him, too. For her own sanity and peace of mind.

It had been fifteen years since they had dated. Fifteen long years of avoiding each other, of ignoring each other. Of pretending the other one didn't exist.

All over one summer fling that could've been so much more.

Whatever. The past didn't matter. The here and now was what mattered. And they were headed to Hafferty's Bar with reports of several injuries from a bar fight.

Who?

How badly were they hurt?

Was one of them Stu?

Would she have to speak to him?

Although they'd had an intense summer affair that had been the highlight of her youth, no one ever knew. They had kept it a secret. She had come home for a visit from college and left back to school with no one the wiser. For a town that thrived on gossip and being in everyone's business, she was surprised no one ever found out she and Stu had been a thing for two short months.

"You okay?" Doug, her partner in crime for the evening, asked as he jerked the ambulance to a stop in the Hafferty's Bar parking lot.

"Besides the rough stop, I'm good," she replied with a chuckle, putting a hand to her neck and mock wincing, although he did love to slam on the brakes too often. She always gave him crap for his terrible driving. He always got a little too eager when a call came through, driving like a bat out of hell and jerking with too much adrenaline coursing through his veins.

"Come on. Ten bucks it's Old Man Rockland causing problems tonight." Doug hopped out and grabbed his medic bag behind the seat.

She grabbed her own and grinned. Old Man Rockland was one of the town drunks—they had a few roaming around—but he was one of them who had a nasty temper when he drank. He usually drank himself into oblivion at home. Sometimes he ventured to the bar, where he normally caused a ruckus and had to have the cops called on him. She wasn't feeling him as the problem maker, though.

She followed Doug, glancing at the patrol car sitting cockeyed near the front door to the bar, its lights flashing.

"Ten says it's Dusty."

Doug grinned and nodded, finalizing the bet, then pulled open the door to the bar.

Light country music played in the background. It didn't mix well with hollering and bellowing coming from—the one and only—Dusty.

She won the bet. Considering she saw him earlier in the day buying a six-pack, she thought it was a pretty good guess that he'd venture to the bar for more drinks. If she hadn't seen him, she would've guessed someone else.

Officer O'Connor was trying to get Dusty to stand up after he handcuffed him, but Dusty didn't want to cooperate —making his body go rigid and refusing to stand. He looked to have a gash on his forehead and a trail of blood on his arm.

Doug looked at her with a frustrated twinkle in his eye —because he lost and owed her ten bucks. Which she'd make him pay. Then his expression turned serious. "I'll take a look at Dusty. You go check out Stu and James." Then he tossed his head toward the bar.

She shifted her attention that way and froze. Just for a second, Stu's eyes met hers. He seemed to tense up.

The past didn't matter; the here and now did.

She had to remind herself of that as she walked toward the two men and closed the distance. James had the look of a decent shiner around his left eye and his cheeks were flushed. Or just red from the scuffle. His bottom lip was also bleeding—he kept touching a white napkin to it.

Stu looked worse. Like Dusty, he also had a large gash to the left side of his head. How bad, she couldn't tell yet, as he was currently holding a large white towel to his head. But she could see the blood soaking through.

"I'm fine."

She paused, opening her medical bag and stared at Stu. Fine. The idiot thought he was fine? He was bleeding from a head wound. He could need stitches. She had no idea until she took a look. But he was definitely not fine.

Well, he was *fine*. The years had been kind to him. As a young man in his twenties, she had been instantly attracted. From his alluring, sexy smile—which she hadn't seen in years—to his golden, hazel eyes that had melted her in her spot the first moment they made eye contact. He'd had longer hair back then. At thirty-five, his hair was short and cropped and framed his face much better than the longer hair had. It let her see his eyes much better. She had always loved looking into his eyes. She had even told him one time they reminded her of the color of whiskey. He had snatched a bottle one time from the bar—when his uncle owned it—and they had a grand time at the lake drinking every last drop.

"Dude, you are not fine. Let her take a look," James said in an incredulous tone, which helped zap her out of her wandering thoughts.

Shit, she had let the past take over for a moment.

She was here. In the present. Here and now. She had to remember that.

"How badly does it hurt? What happened?" she asked with a brisk and professional tone. She could get through this ordeal as long as she kept everything professional.

Stu's eyes flashed fire, then it was as if a cloud of smoke entered and shielded all emotion from her. "Dusty is quite strong for a drunk. He hit me with a barstool. It hurts like hell."

"He was out for a few minutes," James added. "The stool hit him that hard."

She nodded, thankful that James was more forthcoming with information than Stu. She didn't think Stu even wanted to say one word to her, even though she was only here to help him.

Ignoring how much his attitude hurt—how he still wanted to push her away—she got to work. She took his vitals, hating how she had to touch him. He flinched, barely. She flinched slightly in return. His pulse was strong. His reflexes were good. His pupils looked good. He could have a concussion, which she mentioned, and what signs to look out for, especially since he lost consciousness for a few minutes.

Now, the hard part.

"I need to move the towel. By the death grip you seem to have, I hate to have to fight you, but I will." She narrowed her eyes, prepared to exert her dominance in the situation.

His eyes flashed again with an intense fury. At her? She wasn't sure. But then, he masked it once again and dropped his hand slowly from his head.

The gash was small, running across his forehead, near the hairline on his left side. About two inches long, but deep. The bleeding had stopped, probably from the force he'd held the towel to his head. It would require stitches.

Which she proceeded to tell him.

"I can't leave my bar."

She laughed and rolled her eyes. Wow. So, he did care about something in life. His dumb bar.

"Doesn't matter to me if you want to bleed out through the night. Just because it stopped doesn't mean it won't start again. You need stitches, you idiot."

And so much for her professionalism.

His whiskey-colored eyes flashed again.

She was done trying to determine what he was thinking and feeling.

"Phil's here, man. He can take care of the bar for a while. You can always call someone else to help him out. I'll take you to the hospital. It's the least I can do." James glanced at her with a strange look. Then he sighed with defeat. "Well, as long as I don't get arrested, too, I'll take you."

"I won't let them. You didn't do anything wrong." Stu put the towel back to his head, eyeing her a moment, then trained his attention back to James. "Dusty was pushing your buttons and you didn't let him."

"That motherfu—" James inhaled slowly and let out the breath with a patient degree. "I can't believe I was ever friends with him. The shit he was saying about my sister. I feel like an idiot."

"We all make mistakes in life. It's how we fix them that matters."

She wanted to burst out laughing. Was that what Stu thought? Was she a mistake? Was he referring to her? She suddenly wanted to curl up in a corner and cry.

James looked at her for a brief moment, then nodded at Stu. "Let me take you to the hospital."

"Yeah, okay."

"Maybe you should let her bandage up your wound or something," James suggested.

It was her job. Something she was failing at the moment. She should be disinfecting it, wrapping it, and making sure the bleeding had completely stopped. It obviously hadn't since he put the towel back to his head. Yet, she couldn't seem to move her hands toward him.

Stu stood up. She took a step back. He eyed her oddly again.

"I'm fine."

She didn't say anything to his idiotic remark—because he was far from fine, he needed stitches—and watched him walk away toward Officer Crowl, who had arrived. He stood at the bar talking to Phil, the other bartender working tonight.

"Thanks, Chasity," James said softly.

That was odd. What was he thanking her for? She didn't do anything. She certainly didn't do her job.

James followed Stu.

She stood there, letting the past enter her mind once again.

Then she looked around the bar...at the overturned barstools...a table in pieces...glass littered around the floor.

And not one piece of Christmas paraphernalia in sight.

How odd.

It was as if Christmas exploded everywhere around town.

But not in here.

2

"You two don't need to still be here." Stu resisted rolling his eyes, but he was tempted. He felt like Aiden and James were coddling him like a toddler that just received a skinned knee or something.

"Was he this grumpy before the fight, too?" Aiden asked James with a grin.

"Nah, but women can do that to a guy."

Stu whipped his eyes at James. What the hell was he talking about? Aiden beat him to it.

"Oh, do tell. Did I miss something?"

"Maybe Stu can tell us." James gazed at him with a ridiculous grin. As if just because he was happily in love, that meant everyone else around him should be headed in that direction, too.

Not. Happening.

"My head is killing me. The stitches itch. And I want my prescription to be done so I can go home."

Aiden squinted his eyes as if he would find his answer if he looked hard enough.

"The only woman I remember in the bar tonight was

Chasity. Beautiful woman." Aiden looked at James. "Am I right?"

"Yep, she's beautiful. Did not let Stu's cranky attitude bug her either. It was cranky. Never seen that cranky before."

"Dude, you don't even live here anymore and when you did, you weren't around me enough to know when I'm cranky."

Nope.

That woman did not make him cranky.

"Oh, he's vehemently trying to deny it. I think you're on to something here, James." Aiden nodded with a crafty smile and folded his arms.

"You know how they say the air can crackle with this weird kind of energy." James matched Aiden's smile. "It was a crackling and popping as soon as she stepped into his space."

"You two are idiots. You can leave."

He couldn't believe this. He didn't even know James well enough for him to be giving him shit about a woman. And there had been no crackling of any kind with Chasity. Nope. None.

"I have heard that. Not said in that kind of way, but I know what you mean." Aiden pointed at James. "When I first realized Theresa was the one, the air would shift...like with this intensity."

"Yeah, yeah, crackling intensity." James nodded.

"I don't know if crackling is the right word."

"I cannot believe this shit." Stu closed his eyes. Maybe when he opened his eyes, the two of them would have magically disappeared. He'd consider it a Christmas miracle.

"Sizzled," Aiden said, snapping his fingers. "I think I like that word better. The air sizzled with intensity."

Stu popped his eyes open, irritated they were still on this ridiculous conversation.

Aiden grinned at him. James stood next to him with a similar shit-eating grin.

"Is it Chasity that has you in a grumpy mood, Stu?" Aiden asked, lessening the teasing expression in his smile.

"No, it's the stitches in my head, the pounding headache, and you two acting like morons."

Before Aiden or James could continue with their annoying, teasing tirade, Suzanna, one of the nurses who helped Dr. Pearson stitch his wound, stepped into the room with his prescription.

He thanked her, signed the necessary paperwork, and shoved off Aiden's offer to help him stand. He wasn't that hurt. He could walk out of this hospital on his own two feet. Did his head hurt like a son of a bitch from being hit in the skull with a barstool? Yes. Yes, it did. But it wasn't going to stop him from walking or going back to the bar.

Of course, since Aiden had given him a ride to the hospital in his patrol car, he had something to say about his plan.

"Dude, I'm sorry for giving you crap about Chasity. I was trying to make you smile. Dealing with Dusty can bring anyone down. But you can't go back to the bar. You need to go home and rest."

"I'm fine."

"Yeah, I didn't believe that back in the bar, nor do I think Chasity did, and I don't believe you now," James said. His joking expression from inside the hospital had disappeared. Now he looked serious and concerned.

He did not need concern from these two. He was fine. He knew his own body and he. Was. Fine.

"Well, I didn't ask you, did I?"

James's eyes leveled into tiny slits. Stu wasn't worried about him retaliating physically. Maybe a few years ago when he was drinking and getting into trouble all the time, but not now.

Aiden matched James's look and crossed his arms for added effect.

Again, Stu wanted to roll his eyes at their behavior.

It was cold outside as they stood right outside the emergency doors. He only wanted to get a ride to his bar. If they didn't want to help him out, he'd call a cab.

"Don't make me call the chief of police," Aiden finally said as the cold, brutal wind swirled around them.

"Last I checked, I haven't committed a crime. And going back to my bar—a bar I own—isn't a crime either."

"No, it's not, but maybe he can make you see some common sense. He is one of your best friends," Aiden replied with a sharp bite. Almost like the wind as it hit his head, right on his new wound.

Damn it. He didn't want to go home. Nothing waited for him there but silence and the memories. Not the memories he tried to forget around the holidays. No. These memories were worse than that.

Memories of her.

Of sweet, beautiful Chasity.

The one—and only—woman he had fallen in love with.

And then he swiftly broke her heart. His along with it. He had no one to blame for anything that happened between them but him.

He lowered his gaze, pushing a small pile of snow on the sidewalk with his foot. How did he tell them why he didn't want to go home without explaining anything about his past with Chasity? No one had ever known they had one wild summer together. He didn't want to start spreading the word how many years later.

"I'm sure Theresa, Erin, Lynn, and Emma are still baking and stuff. I don't feel like going home yet. I don't mind hanging out if you want company."

Stu looked at James, surprised by his offer. And how well he must've understood his unspoken dilemma.

His head did hurt. His headache wasn't going away, even with the painkiller he took before leaving the hospital. It would be the wiser decision to go home and not to the bar. Phil could handle the rest of the night on his own.

"Yeah, okay." Stu shrugged. "I'd like to hear more about Florida."

"Cool." James nodded at Aiden with a triumphant smile. "I'll see you later at home, after your shift."

Aiden returned a nod with his own beaming smile. "Sounds good." Then he looked at Stu. "Let James stay a while. You could have a concussion, don't forget."

"I'm fine."

He was done talking about his health or anything else— specifically Chasity—with those two. He was fine. How many more times did he have to say it?

James and Aiden shared a look, then Aiden headed to his patrol car while they walked toward James's vehicle.

As James drove him home, his mind drifted to Chasity and how wonderful it had been to see her so close after how many years at a distance. Oh, his eyes always sought her out from a distance. Not that he ever let her catch on that he was staring. He didn't want her to think of him as a stalker or anything. But he couldn't help but seek her out, wonder what she was doing, who she might be doing it with.

She was in his past, though. Something that should stay that way.

Except, it was hard to remember why she should. Why he had made that decision.

He missed her.

Her beautiful ocean blue eyes always sparkled and shined with how she was feeling. She had definitely been irritated with him tonight. Irritated—and angry.

She had every right to be angry with him.

He ruined everything between them.

But he was fine.

Life was fine.

As long as he kept telling himself that lie, everything would remain fine.

———

STRETCHING her neck to the right, then to the left, she gave herself a mental pep talk and then dropped to her knees. She could do this.

She had to do this.

If she didn't do her morning workout routine, she'd regret it. She'd feel lousy all day. Her mental energy would be zapped as well as her physical energy. Working out always put her in a decent mood. Sometimes good. Sometimes okay. Sometimes great. But it always made her happier than not working out.

Except, she had been struggling all morning. She didn't get much sleep last night, tossing and turning, thinking about a man who didn't deserve her thoughts. She woke up feeling groggy and hungover, even though she hadn't had a drop of alcohol.

But she would do this.

Before she changed her mind and ruined her whole day, she started her yoga routine that she could do by memory now. After much searching and following different videos, she managed to create a workout routine that always made her feel rejuvenated for the day. It also helped her maintain her muscle strength and physique. She needed to keep physically fit because there were times she had to lift patients that were double her size.

After doing a good thirty minutes of a combination of yoga and Pilates, she grabbed a quick shower, poured a cup of coffee in a to-go mug, and grabbed her phone. She needed some serious de-stressing with the one person who could always make her see straight.

Her beloved, adorable, sometimes annoying little sister, Hope.

"What's up, Chickadee? Heard there was a bar fight last night."

Chasity had a love-hate relationship with the way her sister could always zero in on the heart of the matter, without even realizing she was doing so.

"Yeah, Dusty causing problems. Stu had to get stitches after getting hit in the head with a barstool. He's so lucky he didn't have more serious injuries." And she was proud of herself for not hesitating on saying his name. She said it as if he meant absolutely nothing to her. As if he hadn't taken her heart years ago and destroyed it into a million pieces.

Or maybe she was blowing it all out of proportion. Young love. Maybe that's all it was and she was making it seem bigger than what it was.

Except she had loved him. She had thought they were on a path to something special...until he told her she wasn't good enough.

"So crazy, all of it. I mean, why was James in the bar in the first place?"

She didn't have a good answer for that. Who was she to

say why someone did what they did? She wasn't about to judge James when she wouldn't want others judging her for some of her outrageous actions.

"No clue. It was an eventful night, that's for sure." Time to move the conversation along. She didn't need her sister to suspect there was more simmering below the surface than what she was portraying. She didn't want to get into her feelings concerning Stu.

"I'm heading to see Grandpa. Wanna join me? Maybe on your lunch break?"

Hope sighed, then whimpered. "Seriously, I wish. Going to work is such a drag. But the gossip of last night's activities has improved the dreary day somewhat. My sister, the hero, saving the day."

Chasity rolled her eyes and chuckled. Her sister was always one for the dramatics. "Oh, please. I showed up after everything was much calmer. I checked some vitals and not much else."

Barely even got that accomplished with how standoffish Stu acted.

"Everything okay at work?"

"Yeah, you know the boss man, always has a stick up his ass, yet portrays to the world he's such a happy, I'm-your-friend kind of guy. The usual. Nothing I can't handle."

Chasity chuckled for her sister's sake, but she didn't think it was funny. Hope worked in the mayor's office—with Stu's dad, who just happened to be the stick-up-his-ass mayor. Not that the town would ever describe him as that. He played a persona to everyone, except in his little corner. He expected his employees to keep it to themselves. And Hope did—except with her. She could always vent to her about anything.

"Well, if I don't see you this week, we're still on for Christmas Day, right?"

Chasity didn't mind working Christmas, and she usually did. Except, this year, her boss insisted she take off, and she didn't argue as it would just be her and her sister around town.

"Of course. Have copious amount of wine ready. Oh, and my present." Hope giggled, then sighed. "Gotta go, I'm needed."

She hung up with her sister, feeling marginally better, even if she hadn't unloaded all her problems concerning Stu with her. Maybe it wouldn't be so wise anyhow. Hope worked for Stu's father, and she never had anything nice to say about him. She might say Stu was just like his dad, which Chasity wouldn't agree with. Not that she had much interaction with Mayor Hafferty, but based on what Hope said about him, Stu was nothing like that. Sure, he broke her heart, but he had been nothing but a gentleman when they dated all those years ago. Plus, the townsfolk loved him. Never heard anything bad said about him. That had to mean something.

With her spirits lifted—albeit still sad, her sister didn't sound particularly happy—she headed out the door. And only twenty minutes behind schedule, as it took longer than she anticipated to give herself a pep talk to work out and having to call her sister.

But she already felt better. Both mentally and physically.

Okay, fine. She didn't get a good night's sleep, but she would not let it ruin her day.

If it weren't for Stu—heartbreaker extraordinaire—she wouldn't have had such a bad night. No matter how hard she tried, she worried about him. She couldn't help herself.

How was he feeling? Did his head hurt? Did he have a concussion?

He seemed very lucid and together—his cold demeanor was enough sign he was of sound mind.

Well, going down that memory lane wouldn't help her, so she wouldn't venture there.

Arriving at her destination, she parked the car and grabbed her coffee before stepping out into the cold. The temperatures were brutal. They felt like last year's temps right before the blizzard hit the town. She hoped they didn't get another one of those. Most people were smart enough to stay home, but some people just didn't have a clue—or care. Blizzards didn't stop her from working. If someone went out on the road and got hurt, she had to go out there as well and help them.

She loved her job. She loved helping people. She simply wished people made better decisions sometimes.

"Hey, Debrah," Chasity said with a smile, waving to her with her free hand.

Debrah returned a smile and waved.

Chasity didn't stop to chat, so Debrah didn't add anything. And if Chasity didn't keep a fluid pace, walking as if she were on a mission, Debrah would slow her down with nonstop chatter. She wasn't a full-blown gossip in town, but she held her own compared to some of the others that couldn't help themselves.

She bypassed her grandpa's room and headed straight for the commons area. They had a small breakfast table set up for the residents along with several tables and chairs, couches, and a nice recliner that everyone took turns sharing.

"Ah, there she is. I was telling these jokers about the time you wrestled a cougar."

Chasity chuckled as she kissed her grandpa's cheek and took a seat next to him. "Why are you telling tall tales?" She wagged her finger at him. "It was a cheetah."

Her grandpa started to laugh. A loud boisterous laugh that always filled her soul with happiness. She visited her grandpa most mornings. Sometimes a quick hello. Sometimes she spent the day. But she enjoyed seeing her grandpa, making him smile, bringing laughter back in his life.

When her mom—his daughter—died five years ago it hit him hard. His only child—gone. Her dad and grandpa had never gotten along, so her dad didn't do much to make him feel better. He didn't even do much to make *her* feel better. Although, he hadn't gotten along with Mom in years, so it was as if he had already mourned her loss.

It shouldn't have landed on her shoulders to make her grandpa feel better, but she took the burden. Hope helped as well, but she tended to work long hours and couldn't always find the time to visit as often as she did. In a way, they helped each other heal and move on from her mother leaving them with such a sudden shock.

A heart attack that no one saw coming.

Another reason she liked to keep in shape—to maintain a healthy lifestyle. She had no idea if she'd befall the same fate as her mother.

"And when did this momentous occasion happen?" Chuck, one of her grandpa's good friends he usually hung out with in the retirement home, said with a silly grin.

"When I went on my African Safari," she said with a deadpan face, then took a sip of coffee.

"She rode on the back of a lion, too." Her grandpa said with all seriousness. But he could only hold it so long, then started laughing again.

She joined in his laughter, his infectious, silly nature

uplifting her spirits. With the added talk with her sister, and now in the presence of her grandpa, all thoughts of Stu disappeared. She knew she could count on her grandpa to make her feel better, without him even knowing he needed to.

"I need more coffee. You need anything, darling?" Chuck asked her as he stood up.

"I'm good." She held up her coffee mug and winked.

Her grandpa waited until Chuck was far enough away before he leveled his concerned grandfatherly stare at her.

"I heard there was a commotion at Hafferty's Bar last night."

She nodded and took a sip of her coffee, hoping he took a hint not to press any further. She didn't want to think about Stu. Not now. Not ever. While she hadn't minded Hope bringing it up, she was done talking about it. She preferred if no one ever brought it up again.

"And?" His brows rose, a quick nod for her to tell him every juicy detail.

She had never confessed to her mother her summer fling with Stu. She hadn't even confessed to any of her friends—not even Hope, which had been odd for her, as she always shared everything with her sister. But somehow, a few years ago when she saw Stu at the grocery store—her grandpa had been with—he got her to confess what had happened between them. She had no idea how he knew something had happened with Stu, but as soon as they returned to her house, he pounced on her, wanting all the details. Wanting her to pour her heart out and make things better. Her grandpa was always wanting to fix things for everyone. He was such a friendly, gregarious guy. Helping people out. Making them feel better. Getting them to laugh, especially at times when they didn't want to. It's the reason she always went out of her way to make him feel better and laugh. She hated it when her grandpa looked sad.

But right now was not a time she wanted to share her feelings about a man she wished she could get over already. Yet, every time she saw Stu, her mind trailed back to that glorious summer. The fun they had. The laughter they shared. The explosive time between the sheets. He was a man hard to forget.

"There's nothing to say. Dusty was causing problems and started a bar fight." She looked down at the table. "Stu got hit in the head with a chair and needed stitches. James and Officer Crowl transported him to the hospital. He's fine, as far as I know. That's it. That's all that happened."

"You talked to him?"

She looked at her grandpa. "Of course. I am a paramedic and it's my job to help people when they're hurt."

He nodded with a small grin. "Maybe it's time you *really* talk to him."

"There's nothing to talk about. We had a thing, like, fifteen years ago. I'm over it." She rolled her eyes as if Stu was nothing more than a distant memory she barely could remember. Even though she dreamt about him more often than she cared to admit.

Fifteen years.

Fifteen stupid years and she couldn't get the man—who had crushed her heart to pieces—out of her mind.

"You're a terrible liar, pumpernickel."

She smiled, despite the depressing topic her grandfather insisted they have. For as long as she could remember, the silly nickname he gave her always made her happy when he said it. It filled her heart with immense joy. Which was funny because he dubbed her that silly nickname after she tried some pumpernickel bread and gagged from how much she hated the taste. Apparently, she made a huge enough commotion to garner the nickname. To this day, she still didn't like pumpernickel bread.

"And you're a nosy old man who's going to get schooled at cards today." She leveled a teasing glare, then grabbed the deck of cards sitting near his side of the table and started to shuffle them.

"We'll see about that." Her grandpa shifted his gaze to something behind her. "I hope you don't mind I invited a new player today."

"Who?"

Then she turned slightly in her chair, the cards in mid shuffle. At the sight of Stu standing in the doorway to the commons area, the cards slipped out of her hands and scattered all over the table.

She whipped her head at her grandpa. "Traitor!"

"You don't get to my ripe old age without a wealth of wisdom, pumpernickel. It's time. Last night should be a good reminder of why it's not healthy to keep our emotions inside. That we let the people we care about know what they mean to us—because I know you still care for him. He could've gotten seriously hurt. What happens if you never get the chance to say what you really feel? How would that make you feel? Not good. I know. We play cards and then you finally talk it out with Stu. Promise me?"

He narrowed his eyes. "Say it. Promise me."

She huffed, her own eyes narrowing. She hated how right he was. "Fine. I promise."

Then his entire face lit up with joy. He waved his hand toward Stu to come join them.

Ignoring the pounding of her heart, she started to gather all the cards together and prepare herself for a very long day.

A chair to her right scraped against the floor.

Stu sat down.

She turned his way. He stared back.

"How's your head feeling?"

She was very proud of how cordial that sounded. Not like she was about to heave last night's contents all over the table.

He looked better today. Although, anyone would look better with blood not trailing down their face. His stitches looked good. Clean and well done. He didn't look pale or withdrawn. He didn't even have the standoffish look in his eyes as he had last night.

"Slight headache, but overall, good."

"Glad to hear." She shuffled once, then two more times.

Then she shot him a wicked smile. Her grandpa said she had to talk it out with him. Fine. She would because she promised and she never broke a promise. But she intended to have as much fun as possible. Because the ensuing talk would likely send her back down the rabbit hole she had to climb out of fifteen years ago.

"We're playing five hundred. Grandpa's my partner. You'll be with Chuck. Do you know the rules?"

"Yep." Stu didn't smile until Chuck sat down across from him and shook hands with him. They exchanged a few pleasantries. Then she dealt the cards out.

"How about we make this interesting?" Her grandpa smiled. One would think it was a smile of an elderly gentleman enjoying the morning with his granddaughter. Chasity knew better. It was a smile with devilish intent behind it.

"Oh, I love interesting," Chuck replied with a chuckle.

"Losers buy the winners dinner. But the winner gets to pick the place."

Chasity sighed. There was no way out of this. Not when it came to her grandpa.

"Splendid idea."

She whipped her head toward Stu, shocked he agreed so quickly. And quite happy about it.

"Great." Her grandpa clapped his hands, the excitement clear.

Oh, yeah.

Just great.

Either way, she lost. She'd be forced to have dinner with a man she couldn't stand anymore. Because every time she saw him, it reminded her of the day he told her he could never love someone like her.

Someone not good enough for him.

3

STU ALMOST LAUGHED out loud at Chasity's suppressed annoyance. Oh, she was smiling, acting like she didn't mind the bet her grandfather just laid down, but he saw the fury blazing in her beautiful oceanic eyes.

He had woken up today with a headache. After taking two pills for the pain, it helped. Two cups of coffee worked a little more. But for some strange reason, the silence had grated on his nerves, more so than usual. So, he decided to visit his grandfather. He was feeling a bit under the weather himself, so Stu didn't stay and chat long. Before he could leave the building, he ran into Roy, Chasity's grandfather.

Although he knew it would be a bad idea, he couldn't refuse the jovial old man when he asked if he wanted to play cards. But he would need his wits about him, so he said he had to use the bathroom first.

He almost hesitated walking toward their table when he saw Chasity. She looked so gorgeous with her blonde hair settled in soft waves on her shoulders. A smile on her face, laughter billowing out at whatever outrageous thing he was sure her grandfather had said.

Yeah, he hesitated. Worried he was making the wrong decision.

But then she turned, and it didn't matter. Not his worries. Not his annoying memories. Nothing mattered but hearing her laugh at something funny he might say. Or seeing her beautiful smile because he put it there.

Fifteen long years.

And his own damn fault.

Seeing her last night. Being so close to her. Actually talking to her. Well, shit, he realized how much he missed her. How much he screwed up.

She wasn't likely to forgive him. They had the most magical summer, then he cut her out of his life as if she hadn't existed. He had done it to protect her. But shit, hindsight was twenty-twenty. In protecting her, he hurt her, so did it make sense what he had done? No. But at the time, a twenty-year-old trying to find his way in life, he thought he was doing the right thing.

So, maybe she wouldn't forgive him. Fine. But it wouldn't hurt to try.

Or maybe he got hit on the head harder than he realized and he was finally losing his mind. No matter the reason, he was moving forward with trying to make amends with the only woman he had ever fallen in love with.

So...

Step one. Play some cards.

Step two. Win or lose, he was getting dinner with her. *Thanks, Grandpa Roy.*

Step three. Apologize.

Step four. Perhaps he'd celebrate Christmas for the first time in over seventeen years, and enjoy it.

He was still undecided on that step. Only if Chasity liked the holiday, which most people did. He wouldn't necessarily say he didn't like Christmas. It was just another holiday in his eyes. He could take it or leave it. But he had his reasons for avoiding it whenever possible.

A feminine voice cleared her throat. "Any day now?"

Stu shook his head and winced at the sudden movement. Damn. He shouldn't jerk his head that way when his headache hadn't completely disappeared yet. But apparently, he had zoned out, letting his thoughts overrun him and didn't realize it was his turn.

Laying the jack of hearts, the right bower down over the ace of hearts Roy laid down, he smiled at Chasity with a "beat that" grin.

"Sorry about that. I was thinking where I want to go out to eat when Chuck and I win."

"I'm a steak man myself," Chuck said with a short laugh.

"You and me both," Stu replied with his own small laugh, but his eyes never left Chasity's.

She tilted her head in the lovable way she always did when she was about to surprise him, usually in a good way —at least that's the way he remembered it. Her lips spread into a wide smile as her eyes sparkled with mischief. He had the intense urge to lean closer and pull her into his arms and kiss her.

Shit. How would she react? What would her grandfather say?

He missed her lips. He missed her laugh. He missed the playful delight that always glittered in her eyes.

Then she laid down the joker over his high card. "I'm more of a seafood fan myself."

"That's my pumpernickel. Never underestimate her."

Stu laughed with Roy, completely agreeing with the sentiment.

The game continued with merry fun. They all enjoyed

teasing each other with who was going to win and who would lose. Surprisingly, he didn't sense any tension between him and Chasity. Well, maybe a bit of tension. But not the angry kind.

Unless he was the only one feeling the sexual pull between them.

Every time they connected eyes, he wanted to inch closer and kiss her. Devour her mouth and not come up for air for days.

The game took longer than he anticipated. Although, when he left his house this morning, while he didn't expect to be gone this long, he also hadn't expected to spend the morning with Chasity. He wasn't regretting his decision to leave the house.

But some regret was filling him up.

Just a different kind. The one from fifteen years ago. For acting like a colossal ass and creating a distance that wasn't necessary.

When Chasity pulled the last trick her way, signaling she and Roy won the last round, which put them over 500 points, he knew he lost the game. But he still won in the end. He still had a dinner to look forward to.

"Well, darn. I can never win a game against Roy. It's just not fair," Chuck grumbled, but in a teasing way.

"And you never will," Roy said matter-of-factly.

"I have to get going," Chasity said as she stood up from her chair and then leaned closer to Chuck and planted a light kiss to his cheek. "I'll bring you takeout from Genevieve's later tonight. A nice juicy steak and mashed potatoes. Your favorite."

"You sure know a way to a man's heart. But losers buy the winners dinner." Chuck hugged her before she backed away.

"Well, you give me the money and I'll deliver it to you. Remember, Grandpa said the winner gets to pick the place. They have the best shrimp scampi on the planet. So, we both get what we want," Chasity replied.

"And me?" Stu chimed in.

He suddenly wasn't liking where she was going with this.

"I'll deliver the steak to you as well. You can pay me what you owe me. I'll drop it off at the bar."

That wasn't how this was supposed to work.

"I thought we'd go out to eat."

"But we don't have to."

"And if I wanted to?"

Chasity froze, her face morphing into shock as if someone just puked on her brand-new shoes.

He sensed Roy and Chuck glancing between the two of them, but he didn't remove his gaze from her. Shit. He was shocked himself those words came out of his mouth. But damn it. He wanted to make amends and Roy had produced the perfect way to do that. With dinner. And now she was trying to change the rules of the game.

Getting knocked in the head with a barstool was the best thing that happened to him in a long time. It finally made him see what he had been missing in his life.

Her.

It was way past time he did something about it.

Chasity mysteriously smiled. "Grandpa said losers buy the winners dinner. Not *take* them out to dinner. You get steak and I'll drop it off at the bar later."

Then she circled the table, kissed her grandfather on the cheek, and waltzed out of the room like she hadn't just tilted his entire world off its axis.

"Hmm. I didn't see that one coming."

Stu glanced at Roy and arched a brow. "What?"

"Don't 'what' me, son." Roy wagged a finger in his face. "I know there's history between you two. I just gave you a nugget. So don't go and screw it up. The rest is up to you." Then he leaned closer. "But you hurt my pumpernickel again and I'll hurt you. Got it?"

Oh, he got it.

Roy was one of the favorite people in town. One word from him, and his business wouldn't see, well, much business. Considering it was the only bar in town, that was saying a whole lot.

What an interesting turn of events. Roy knew the history between him and Chasity. He was, oddly enough, trying to help him out. How much did he know? What had she told him?

How did he turn this situation with the small nugget thrown his way into his favor?

Roy narrowed his eyes, waiting for confirmation he understood what was at stake.

"I got it. Thanks for the game." He stood up. "And the nugget."

Roy sat back in his chair and smirked at Chuck as if sharing a secret he wasn't privy to. "Some say there's magic in the air around this town during the holidays. Someone's always getting engaged or falling in love."

Well, Stu didn't think that would happen between him and Chasity. It would take more than magic. It'd take a Christmas miracle.

Perhaps he'd write a letter to Santa. Because he suddenly wanted a Christmas miracle.

He wanted Chasity back.

"I've never believed in magic."

Hell, he didn't even believe in Santa anymore. No miracles coming his way. What a silly thought to even write to the old guy in red.

"Doesn't mean magic doesn't believe in you," Roy countered.

What an odd thing to say. He didn't know what it meant. And it didn't matter. What mattered was thinking of the right words to say when he saw Chasity again.

Because saying "I'm sorry" didn't seem like enough.

OKAY, so she won the game of cards, but that didn't mean she had to completely play by her grandpa's rules. She'd pick up the meal and Stu could reimburse her. The less she had to deal with the man, the better.

It had played hell on her nerves to sit at the same table with him after so many years of keeping her distance.

All those memories—wonderful memories at the time —flooded her system. They didn't seem so wonderful after his painful words crushed her right afterward.

So, yeah, she'd honor the dumb bet, but on *her* terms.

She ordered four meals from Genevieve's before her shift started and picked it up within thirty minutes. Mulberry didn't have a fancy restaurant like Genevieve's, so she had to run to Mason to pick it up. She didn't mind going a little out of her way because they seriously made the best gourmet meals around these parts.

She dropped the two meals off to her Grandpa and Chuck, almost refusing to accept Chuck's money. But she couldn't. Because if she did, she'd have to do the same with Stu, and she didn't want to. A bet was a bet and they lost.

They suggested she eat with them, but she had to get to

work. Her shift would start soon and she had never been late to work in her life. She wouldn't start now. Although, that did pose a problem dropping off Stu's meal. Unfortunately, he'd have to heat it up, just like she'd have to do with hers.

She had every intention of dropping his meal off during her break, but her shift turned out busier than usual. The roads became icy from a light misting rain, then the temperatures dropped significantly, which impacted the roads. She and Doug barely had time to scarf down some granola bars they kept in the ambulance with them.

By the time her shift ended at eleven, she was ready to go home and crawl into bed. Except, she hadn't delivered Stu his meal, and she wanted to get it over with.

She saw a few cars in the parking lot, recognizing Stu's truck parked on the side of the building. Of course, she figured he'd be at work. He generally was. Not that she made a note to seek his truck out or what he might be up to. Nope. Not her.

Releasing a slow breath, she grabbed the bag that held his cold steak and the best garlic mashed potatoes on the planet and exited the car. Pulling open the door to the bar, she made a quick cursory glance. The bar was nearly empty with only about five people besides Stu standing behind the bar with Chris, another bartender on duty tonight.

Their gazes met.

He looked frozen in place. His arm outstretched with a rag in his hand, wiping down the counter.

They stared at each other for a moment.

Then she moved forward, deciding they wouldn't get anywhere staring at each other. That jolted Stu out of his stupor, as he stood straighter and let go of the rag.

"Hey, I brought your food." She lifted the bag. "Sorry I'm so late and that it's cold. It was a busy night."

She couldn't hold in the sigh that escaped. It had been a *very* busy night. More exhausting than most and she wasn't sure why. Maybe because she knew she'd eventually have to deal with Stu and she didn't want to.

"I'm sorry to hear that." He relaxed his stance.

She could tell he was being sincere. Although, she wasn't sure why she expected him to be rude or anything. He was a perfect gentleman this morning when they played cards.

Maybe because she couldn't dispel the memory of him telling her they were done. Finished. Never gonna happen.

She set the bag on the counter. "Glad to see it's not busy here." Then she looked horrified and embarrassed. "Not that I want your bar to not get business. That's not what I meant. I meant because the roads are very icy. People shouldn't be out and about."

Her car had even fishtailed a few times on her way to the bar. Thankfully, it was on her way home; otherwise, he would've been waiting another day for his meal.

He grinned and pulled out his wallet. "I knew what you meant. I might shut the bar down early. Elliot stopped by and told me how bad the roads are getting. How much do I owe you?"

The smile appeared before she could suppress it. "Fifty-five dollars and thirty-two cents, but you can keep the change if you'd like."

His mouth formed in a wide circle, then he opened his wallet and fished out three twenties. "It's a good thing I know they have great steak. Not bad for four meals either."

She pushed the bag toward his side of the bar and took the money he had set down. "Oh, that was only for your meal and mine. Chuck paid for his and Grandpa's meal."

He chuckled. "Now I remember why I rarely eat at Genevieve's." He started to open the bag. "Keep the change."

She stopped digging in her purse for her wallet. It was five dollars. Not that much money. Not enough to argue with him about. So, she nodded and fixed the strap of her purse on her shoulder. "Have a good night. Drive safe."

Then she turned around and headed for the exit.

"Chasity, wait."

Her steps slowed.

"Join me."

She turned his way.

He waggled two boxes, one in each hand with an adorable grin on his face.

Well, shit.

She forgot to take her meal out of the bag. Did she want to be in his presence any longer than she had to be? Yes. Maybe. Sort of.

She promised her grandpa she'd talk to him, too. Not that she was prepared to have that sort of conversation tonight.

It was terrible to want to stay, and a very bad decision. This man had taken her heart and filled it with love and joy and then promptly crushed it and crumbled it until it was nothing more than a grain of dust.

His grin fell away, then he stretched out one of the boxes toward her. "You don't have to. I thought it would be...maybe we could...talk."

Not good. His stumbling of words suggested he wanted to talk about things that should be left in the past.

Again, her grandpa's promise filtered in her head. She hated how much sense her grandpa had made. They did need to talk. Because her heart had never fully healed. Every time she went on a date, which wasn't too often, she always compared them to Stu. And she knew that was completely unfair to the guy. Dating in a small town was a real struggle. Finding men outside of their small town was too hard. Dating just sucked; she tried to avoid it.

"Okay. I didn't really get a decent meal tonight." Her stomach took the opportunity to voice its agreement.

They both chuckled at the loud grumbling noise.

She took a seat at the bar as Stu headed behind two swinging doors that led to the small kitchen. In the few short minutes he was gone, she argued back and forth with herself on how bad of an idea this was. Sometimes rehashing the past didn't go well. It only opened up old wounds and doused them with more pain.

She glanced around the bar again, noting the few patrons still in attendance. Thankfully, a few older gentlemen not likely to spread gossip. The last thing she needed was rumors floating around town that she and Stu were a thing. Considering Stu wanted to keep their relationship a secret years ago, he wouldn't appreciate rumors starting and flying around like the brisk, cold wintery night.

But sometimes talking mended old wounds. Healed them enough to move on. Sure, a scar still lived, but the pain ebbed away.

Stu came through the swinging doors with two white plates filled with delicious smelling food. He had his steak with mashed potatoes, green beans, and a dinner roll they handmade every day. Her plate was piled high with large shrimp she knew would taste fresh and delicious on a hill of angel hair pasta and the best sauce she'd ever had.

He set the plates down and pushed hers closer to her.

Then they both dug in.

They both must've been hungry because neither spoke as they chowed down. Before long, her plate was a third cleared—she could never eat the entire meal—and his was almost devoid of any food.

The silence had been pleasant as they ate. As his fork clinked onto his plate, the silence turned tense. Thick and dense tension.

He inhaled deeply, then looked at her. "I'm sorry."

She should've shielded her reaction, but she couldn't stop the slight jolt his words had on her. She flinched, her brows pleating together.

"What?"

He stood taller as he had been leaning down on the bar and ran a hand through his hair, wincing a little when he hit his stitches on the side of his head.

"I acted like an ass all those years ago, and I'm sorry. You didn't deserve the way I treated you. I know it doesn't make up for my behavior, and I should've apologized a long time ago, but I'm sorry."

Wow.

Okay.

Her heart still hurt from the lost love she thought she could've had with him, but oddly enough, his apology filled just a little bit of the hole from his hurt.

"I'm sorry, too."

A slow, seductive grin emerged. Oh, she could never resist his grins. The way his mouth moved sensuously as if telling her with his lips what he was about to do. "Why are you sorry? I broke things off with you."

She shrugged as her own mischievous smile appeared. "I called you some pretty nasty words. I mean..." She rolled her eyes and giggled. "...not to your face, but I feel compelled to apologize for them."

"Well, I deserved them." He laughed.

More silence developed between them. Awkward

silence. Not the icky tension from before but a slight tension, nonetheless.

It was time for her to get out of here before she did something stupid. Like, fall into his arms once again.

Not happening.

She learned from her mistakes.

This should be enough to fulfill the promise she made to her grandpa. They talked. They apologized. They could move on now.

"Thanks for the meal." She stood up and started to put on her coat.

"Thanks for delivering it." He frowned, then produced a smile. "We never had dessert."

Oh, dessert.

Just what kind of dessert was he talking about?

She zipped up her coat. "That wasn't part of the bet."

He nodded. "New bet, then? Loser buys the winner dessert."

What game was he trying to play now? But she was too much of a chicken to come straight out and ask him. Not tonight, anyway. She was exhausted and tired from work, and she'd be exerting more mental energy on the drive home to stay on the road.

"Another game of cards?"

He shook his head. "No, I think we both know you'd school me on that again."

She grabbed her purse from the counter. "Then what do you have in mind?"

"Meet me tomorrow morning around ten at Dragon Hill. Dress warm." The wicked, teasing devils in his eyes said she'd have fun, but most likely regret it.

"Fine." Then she positioned her purse on her shoulder. "But I'm not a fan of surprises, which you know from fifteen years ago. I'll play one more game with you, Stu, but I won't be giving you my heart again."

Then she walked out into the frigid cold, knowing she was going to regret every moment forward.

Because she lied. He already had her heart. But maybe somehow, she could get it back from him and remove him from her memories completely.

4

THE WIND WHIPPED around him as he waited for Chasity to arrive.

She was late.

Not too late, but late. About ten minutes. He didn't think he could use the knowledge he had of her from fifteen years ago because a person could change. Because when he went through his memories—something he tried hard not to do —he didn't remember her ever being late to meet him.

Which didn't bode well for his chances. She changed her mind.

Last night had been unexpected. He had enjoyed her company. Although, he always had. They hadn't talked much, besides his lame apology. He didn't think simple words would help show her how truly sorry he was for hurting her, but it was a start. Even though they hadn't conversed much, he had enjoyed being in her presence. He forgot how much he liked being near her.

As he looked back at his reasons for pushing her away, they were dumb. The decisions of a punk kid who didn't have a backbone. That was the only excuse he had.

Well, that, and he didn't want any negativity to touch her life like it touched his whenever he was in his father's presence. Just thinking about the guy brought his mood down.

Yeah, so what was his excuse for continuing to stay away from her when he finally found the strength to take charge of his life? To not let his father think he could control him.

He was a moron. No way around it.

He knew she wouldn't give him a second chance. A part of him said he shouldn't even try. Her life would turn to hell, just as he lived on occasion.

Another gust of wind slapped him in the face, shaking him out of a dangerous rabbit hole he didn't want to fall in. Not now. Not later. Not ever.

He adjusted his hat, wincing when the material scraped against his stitches. The area was still tender, but his head didn't pound like a stampede of elephants was running over him.

Pushing his jacket up slightly to check his watch, he sighed.

She wasn't coming. She backed out. He would've sworn she wouldn't be able to resist another bet. Her eyes had flashed a brilliant blue yesterday when her grandpa suggested the first bet, as if she couldn't resist a challenge.

Apparently, with him, she could.

I'll play one more game with you, Stu, but I won't be giving you my heart again.

Her parting words as she left the bar. It reinforced how much he hurt her.

Well, he had hurt, too. It wasn't as if he wanted to break things off with her. He hadn't wanted to keep their fling a secret either, but...

Yeah, the damn but. Just an excuse for him having no backbone.

From this day forward, he would not use that word anymore. No more buts. He'd say what he meant without using an excuse. He was a grown man and he had to start acting like one.

He sighed again, a large plume of cold air circling his face.

Shit, it was cold out.

This was a bad idea anyway, especially with a recent head injury.

He closed his eyes, feeling the chilly wind hit his face, hating that she stood him up.

He deserved it.

"Sorry I'm late. I had to work out because if I don't work out, it throws my whole day off."

His eyes popped open to see Chasity standing in front of him. Her cheeks were a rosy red, most likely from the wind. He imagined his cheeks were bright red as well. His nose felt like it was about to fall off.

She had on a white knitted hat and a big fluffy white knitted scarf wrapped around her neck. She looked beautiful. Like an angel sent from heaven. Like a Christmas gift he hadn't asked for. Not that he ever asked for any gifts. His mother always bought him some, though. Slapped his father's name onto it as if he had helped pick it out. Which he never did. Stu wasn't naive.

"No problem. I guess I could've told you to skip the workout because you'll be getting one here."

Her brows puckered. "I never skip my workout. What do you have in mind? Why are we here?"

He couldn't suppress a giddy grin as he turned and pointed up the big hill behind him. Dragon Hill. Aptly named because it was a beast to climb.

"We're going sledding."

Her mouth opened, shocked. Then she glanced down at his feet where a wooden sled sat, then her eyes trailed to the hill.

"A sledding race? With one sled?"

His grin widened. "Not exactly a race."

This was probably the worst, dumbest bet on the planet. When it popped out of his mouth last night, he wasn't sure what he had in mind. Only that he wanted another moment with her, even if it was a silly excuse. This morning when he ventured into his garage and saw his sled, he still didn't know what kind of bet he'd offer her, but he grabbed it and headed out the door.

He was totally winging everything here.

"Just what exactly?" Her lips were in a tight line, but on her, it looked adorable—like she was trying to appear mad, but also intrigued to know more. Her eyes were definitely sparkling with interest.

"When's the last time you've taken a jaunt down Dragon Hill on a sled?" For him, when he was sixteen-years-old. A long time.

He was a bit nervous if he was being honest. Not that he was about to share that honesty with her. He certainly didn't want to look like a wuss.

She removed her irritated gaze from him and looked at the hill again.

Kids loved to sled down Dragon Hill. It was steep. It had bumps and curves. It whipped you down the hill in break-neck speeds. Although kids loved it, parents weren't always a fan. Too many broken bones and mishaps that led to less and less sledding. He knew teenagers around the town still came here for fun. These days, people used it with snow-boards and skis, rather than sleds. A little less dangerous.

"I've never been sledding here."

No way.

"Seriously?" A soft chuckle escaped as his grin widened. Well, not only would this be an interesting bet, but he'd get her to experience something new.

"It's cold as shit out here. I'd rather be cuddled up under a blanket reading a book than playing outside in the snow." She didn't return a smile.

"Well, you're here, so let's have some fun." Shit. He needed to tell her what the bet was. Which was...he had no clue.

So, he said the first thing to pop into his head. "We take a stroll down the hill on the sled. The person to stay on the sled until the end wins."

Her eyes rounded into large saucers as she looked at the hill once more. "The fact you're making that as a bet has me concerned. You do have a head injury from two days ago, you know. It's not the best thing to be doing right now."

It touched his heart, filling up the lonely ache that had dwelled there for far too long. She cared if he got hurt or not. He was a little concerned about falling off as well. But not enough to back out now.

"My head's feeling fine. It'll be fun. I promise you'll have fun."

Her entire expression fell into despair. The pain echoed in her bright blue eyes, as beautiful as the bright crystal blue sky. Her lips formed a frown that took the happiness she just filled his heart with and wiped it clear.

Shit.

What did he say to make her look like all her Christmas presents magically disappeared from under the tree?

Wow. It was as if she was transported back in time. Twenty years old, full of life and fun and new adventures. Wanting to learn and advance in a field where she couldn't wait to help people. Not that she was bitter and unhappy now at thirty-five years old, but life and her feelings had been different back then.

I promise you'll have fun.

How many times had he said that to her that summer? So many times, she lost count. Oh, and she always had fun.

He usually said it right before he wanted her to do something ridiculously crazy. Like, jump off high rocks—more like a cliff—at the quarries. A person couldn't see below the surface of what was hiding. Rocks. Fish. Just water. Tons of kids jumped off the rocks at the quarries. No one ever got hurt. Well, not hurt that badly. No one ever died there that she knew.

It was crazy, though. She wasn't even a fan of heights. Yet, the slight dare in his eyes. The smooth smile that everything would be okay. The giddy feeling of love.

She jumped.

She screamed.

She survived.

She had followed him like a lovesick fool into every crazy thing he insisted would be fun. Promised would be fun. He never broke that promise.

But he sure broke her heart.

"I'm sorry."

She tore her eyes away from the hill straight to his forlorn eyes.

"For what?"

He shrugged. "For whatever put that look on your face. I'm sorry."

Each time those two simple words came out of his

mouth, they sounded more and more real. Like he *was* sorry for hurting her.

It didn't mean she would trust him with her heart.

She looked at the hill again, the wind biting her cheeks.

Ugh. She could never resist a challenge.

"Let's do this. Loser buys the winner dessert."

A wide, beaming smile split across his lips. "The first one to the top gets to pick who sits where."

Then he snatched up the sled and started running up the hill. She followed behind him and quickly understood what he meant by this could've been her workout. Running at the intense pace they were, up a very steep—long—hill was not as easy as it seemed.

About midway, they both started to slow down. He was still ahead of her by a few extra steps. Although, she planned to argue if he won that he cheated, which he had. He took off before giving her a chance to know what was about to happen. Not fair.

Of course, life wasn't fair. It taught her that over and over as time went on.

What did she do each time unfairness was thrown in her face?

She persevered. She kept moving on. She put an extra pep in her step to show she would not let anything, or anyone, get her down.

That surge of motivation that always internally spiked when she most needed it, got her to the top of the hill before him. By two steps.

But a win was a win.

"Nice race," Stu said, breathing heavily, resting his hands on his knees as he tried to regain his breath.

She wasn't faring any better, and instead of getting her breath back like him, she plopped down onto her butt on the cold snow. Then she laid back and looked up at the bright blue sky, not a cloud in sight.

It looked like it was going to be a beautiful day, albeit cold.

She felt Stu near her immediately. Turning her head away from the pretty picture above, she met Stu's eyes right next to her.

"I got some snow inside my shoe."

She giggled because she knew she got some inside hers. Geez. He said to dress warm. He didn't say to dress in snow pants, boots, and all the paraphernalia one needs to go sledding.

"This was your idea."

His eyes, which sparkled like the golden sun above, glittered with sudden desire. "Best idea I had all week."

Oh, no.

Nope.

She would not fall for his charm again. Fifteen years ago, he ripped her heart out. Hadn't she learned from her mistakes?

"Because I love dessert." His lips split into a delicious smile that said he wanted dessert right this second.

"Well," she said as she sat up, "you better hope you win; otherwise, you don't get to pick the kind of dessert you want. You might not like what I pick."

He sat up as well. "I love all kinds of dessert. I'm honestly not picky."

"We'll see."

She intended to win, and she was tempted to pick the most off-the-wall dessert there was. Something that would have him hesitating to try. Lynn, who ran Sweet Treat Delights, always had an amazing array of yummy goodies. Even if Lynn didn't have something stocked, she figured if she asked Lynn nice enough, she'd make whatever it was she decided.

Stu stood up and extended his hand. She hesitated, but only for a second. While she wanted to limit contact with him, it would only make her look like a bitch to refuse his help to stand. When her gloved hand connected with his, sparks sizzled between them. She could feel it right down to her skin.

He helped her stand and she immediately retreated from his touch. She would not fall into the same trap again. She would not let him woo her, make her believe things might be real this time, only to have him break her heart with a few simple words.

"You won the first race. Do you want to sit in the front or back of the sled?" Stu asked as he positioned the sled.

She looked out over the horizon. They were on the north side of town. She could see the steeple from the church. Snow covered the ground and treetops, making it look very serene and picture-perfect—a sweet, little town nestled in a quiet area. She lived in town, in a small apartment building that held only ten residents. It was very quiet. Her apartment was on the first floor, yet she never heard footsteps or pounding or loud noises coming from above. It was nice. Although Charlie, who worked for the fire department and had the same shift as hers, lived above her, so it made sense he wasn't loud. He slept when she slept. He was gone when she was gone. He was a quiet guy in general anyway.

Then her eyes trailed down the large hill. From way up here, it looked steep. She climbed the beast. She knew how steep it was. But looking down from high above, it looked worse. Like if she fell off, it would hurt.

It hadn't snowed in four days. The snow that was on the ground was almost packed to the earth, which created a slick path. It wasn't fluffy and light where it would break her fall if—or when—she crashed.

So, the million-dollar question: would she be more likely to fall off sitting in front, or back?

The person in front would probably have more leverage to steer the sled. But the person in the back would more than likely be able to stay on better.

She didn't think Stu would purposely steer the sled wrong if he was the driver because if he fell off, he'd lose.

She thought, anyway. She honestly wasn't sure as she had never gone sledding in her life. Growing up, she was more of a bookworm than an outdoorsy person. Her sister Hope had been to Dragon Hill. By her outrageous stories, she knew it wasn't something she'd enjoy. So, she never went.

Producing a smile, ready to get this fun started, she replied, "I'll sit in back."

Stu eyed her critically for a moment, then nodded. As if deducing the same things she concluded in her mind.

He sat down first, scooting his butt toward the front of the sled, but leaving enough room for her in the back. She took her position as well, her heart suddenly pounding when she scooted closer to him.

He twisted his head with a devilish grin. "You're going to have to hold on to me." His wicked grin intensified. "Or you'll fall off and lose."

"I rarely lose." She shifted closer and wrapped her arms around his waist. She was not afraid of a challenge, even one that had her body singing with desire. "I hate losing."

"Hold on tight, sweetheart."

Before she could give him a tongue lashing for calling her an endearment he had no right to call her, he pushed his feet against the ground and they were off.

Sure, she had wrapped her arms around his waist, but not tightly. As soon as she felt the wind on her face, a small squeal left her mouth and her arms gripped him like a vice holding a project together full of sticky glue.

The wind was brutal, hitting her face like a sharp slap on the cheek, one after another. Repeated blows that sent tingles of pain down her spine. A small spray of snow pelted her face as well.

Yet, the rush in her veins. The hard body wrapped in her arms. The laughter coming from in front of her, had her joining his laughter.

This was fun.

She'd never been sledding in her life.

What a thrill.

They were making headway down the long hill, picking up speed as they went. She assumed because the snow was packed down. Not good, especially if they tumbled.

It came out of nowhere. A tiny bump in their pathway. A small little elevation they hit just right.

The sled went airborne. Not truly high, but enough where her laughter turned to a shriek.

It had to have been no more than a second, but it was enough to startle her when they hit the ground. It startled Stu as well.

The sled jerked a fraction to the right, which threw off their momentum.

They both tumbled off the sled together. Her cheek scraped the side of the hill, cold snow rubbing her face and sending a chill straight down her spine. She even tasted a bit of wet snow in her mouth.

Talk about a face plant right into a snowy tundra.

Her body hurt in a few places from hitting the ground a bit harder than she anticipated. She hadn't been prepared to fall off. It came too suddenly. But she didn't think she had broken anything.

She gazed at the bright blue sky once again. Such a beautiful sight. Then a large shadow blocked her view. It morphed into Stu's handsome face. He was lying right next to her.

"We both fell off." He smiled.

"Well, you shifted us the wrong way, which makes it your fault, which means I won."

His eyes glittered with the same desire when they were at the top of the hill. "Is that right?"

"Yep." She emphasized the 'p' as it left her mouth, with a sort of pop to the end of it.

"I call rematch."

"You can't just—"

Then his lips were on hers, cutting off any rebuttal she wanted to make.

Warm, sweet lips she had missed.

5

HE HAD GOTTEN a face full of snow, which had been more of a shock to the system than he anticipated when he tumbled off the sled. Now, with his lips morphing with Chasity's, his body was in overdrive. Everything tingled. The good kind of tingles that he had missed.

He didn't even know what possessed him to kiss her. Other than the fact he wanted to. He'd been dying to kiss her since the moment she walked into his bar two nights ago, even if he was just admitting it to himself.

Her arms wound around him, pulling him closer.

Definitely not the response he expected from her, but he wouldn't complain. He deepened the kiss. Nothing mattered but her lips melting with his. Not the bite of the wind hitting his cheeks. Not the snow that somehow snuck inside his coat around his neck. Not how much his feet felt like they were about to fall off. Shit. This had been his idea and he didn't even wear his snow boots.

He could kiss her forever.

Damn it.

And he couldn't. She wasn't his. She'd never be his

because he had screwed it up years ago, and not much in his life had changed to make a go of things now.

Hating it with every breath in his body, he forced himself to detach himself from her. A low, achy moan echoed between them. Then she popped open her eyes, and although her moan betrayed how she felt, she plastered an annoyed glare to her face.

"Why did you kiss me?"

He swore since the day he lied to her, he'd never lie again. Not to her, at least.

"Because I couldn't help myself. Because I wanted to."

The sternness in her expression changed into sadness.

Not a look he wanted to see.

"Well, resist next time. Please get off me."

He wanted to pout like a little boy not getting a piece of candy from his stocking. Instead of having a toddler tantrum, he did as she requested. Then he stood up and held out his hand to assist her.

She cocked a brow and stared at his hand. It took her a few seconds before she finally slid her hand into his. He helped her stand. He used a little more force than necessary because he jerked her to her feet, and the momentum sent her into his chest. She had to put her free hand out to stop herself.

He clutched her hand tighter and wound an arm around her waist.

Her eyes leveled into tiny slits.

"Just because we're standing doesn't mean I give you permission to hold me."

"I miss holding you."

Her eyes drew downward. "Don't do this, Stu. You had your chance."

Shit. He knew that. He knew he blew his chances all

those years ago. But he wanted another chance. Having her in his arms after such a long absence was making all those precious memories flood back into his system. Memories he forced himself to forget. Memories he told himself he didn't need.

"I was an idiot back then. I made a mistake."

He increased his grip on her hand. He could sense she wanted to pull away, and honestly, as a gentleman, he should let her. But he wasn't feeling particularly gentlemanly at the moment.

She lifted her eyes. "You told me I would never be good enough for you."

"What?" His entire body jerked at her words. "I never said that."

"You did." Then she shoved at his hand and pushed away from him.

He didn't fight her. He wouldn't fight her. Not physically. Not ever. But he would fight *for* her. Because he never once said she wasn't good enough. Hell, if anything, he wasn't good enough for her, especially after the way he pushed her away and ended things so abruptly.

He couldn't stand the ache in her eyes. Turning away from her, he grabbed the sled's rope and threw a smile on his face he didn't feel.

"I still call rematch."

She pursed her lips. "You lost."

"We both fell off."

"I'm okay with that. It's a tie then. We both lost."

Then she started walking down the hill at a bit of a sideward angle so she didn't fall.

Well, that was that. He screwed up again.

He didn't follow after her, figuring she didn't want him to. She wanted nothing to do with him. When she made it to her car and got in and shut the door, he cursed himself for not running after her.

Idiot. Again.

He should've run after her. He should've declared his intentions. That he wanted to try again. That he wanted to show her he could be the man she deserved.

He took his own time climbing down the hill, slipping and tripping a few times before making it down the hill without falling flat on his ass. The sled made a loud clunking noise after he threw it into the back of the cab of his truck. He drove the long way home, going over everything that happened. How he could've done it differently. Where it might've gone wrong.

Most likely the kiss screwed it all up. He should've kept his lips to himself.

When he got home, he showered, changed into new clothes, and decided to make a light lunch. As he was about to take a bite of his ham sandwich, a light knock sounded on his door.

Hope swelled inside.

Maybe Chasity had a change of heart. Maybe she wanted to try once more like he did.

The hope died when he opened the door to his mom.

"Oh, you look a bit pale. Are you resting like the doctor ordered?" his mother asked as she stepped inside, patting his cheek in the way she always did when he was sick.

Not that he was sick. But he had suffered a minor injury a few days ago, and his mother could hover like a momma cat with a new litter of kittens.

"I'm fine, Mom. I've been taking it easy." Besides the whole sledding incident where he could've hurt himself falling off the sled in the wrong way. But he wasn't going to share any of that or whom he'd been with. Not that his mother had a problem with Chasity. Everyone in town liked Chasity. She was a very friendly, outgoing woman. Most people liked her. Most men loved to ogle her. At least, from what he noticed when she was in his vicinity, something he tried to avoid at all costs. Because he hated reminders that he lost her. At his own stupidity.

"Have you?" She pierced her eyes in the way she always did when she didn't believe him.

Which made him wonder what she might've heard. Had someone seen him and Chasity at Dragon Hill and immediately reported it to his mother? It wouldn't surprise him with the way gossip spread around town.

"Yes." Then he grinned and headed for the kitchen. He wasn't about to elaborate and invite more questions about the matter of his health. "Do you want me to make you a sandwich? I just made myself one for lunch."

"Oh, no, dear, but thank you. I had lunch with your father at work. I wanted to check on my son."

In other words, she wanted to hover and make sure her *only* son was healthy and strong and taking care of himself in the way she wanted him to.

"I'm fine, Mom. I promise," he replied as genially as he could, then sat down at the table.

His mother also took a seat.

"We missed you at the Christmas party. Everyone asked about you."

Sure, they did. Everyone knew he never attended the dumb annual Christmas party. Only his parents, especially his father, expected him to attend. Every year, without fail, he didn't attend—no matter how much his father berated him for it.

Everyone always brought presents to be donated to all the children around the local hospitals. Although he never showed up, he always donated directly to the fire station, who delivered all the presents with their firetruck.

"I hope you had a good time."

And he did. He would never wish his mother to have a bad time. His father…he could rot in hell, for all he cared.

"We're having a small Christmas Eve party. We're hoping you'll attend." She added a beaming smile as if that would persuade him.

The two of them did this every year. She would ask. He would decline. She'd get sad and upset. He'd apologize. She'd plead her case once more. He'd decline. She'd mention his father. He'd get upset. She'd leave upset. He'd feel like a terrible son, apologizing one more time, but ultimately, not going to the party.

He pushed his sandwich away, his appetite diminished. Even after his mother left, he knew he wouldn't take a bite.

"Can we not do this, Mom? Can we not argue and get upset at each other?" He pleaded with his eyes for her to hear him. "We both know the only reason he wants me at these parties is to try and change my mind and follow in his footsteps. He uses the holiday as an excuse to get me close to him. It's not happening. I'm happy. I like my life. I like the bar. I like being me. What is so wrong with me just being me?" He sat straighter, not pausing in his tirade. "If you wanted to invite me to a Christmas party that didn't involve any political nonsense, I'd attend. But it'll never happen, so I'll never attend."

And he'd spend Christmas alone—for the umpteenth time—and have a very merry Christmas, despite what people might think. He didn't hate the holiday. He hated the pressure his father always tried to put on him to change his lifestyle to his way of thinking.

His mother stood up, no smile, no sadness, only plain

coolness displayed. It didn't surprise him. As the wife to the mayor, she had developed a persona for the world to see. If she didn't want them to see something, she hid it behind a cool facade.

Then she reached across the table and brushed her hand on his cheek as she had done in the foyer.

"There's nothing wrong with you being you. I love you. I wish the two men in my life could stop fighting. It's tiring. And it's almost Christmas, and just once, I wanted my son in my house for the holidays. Not stopping by to drop off a present and leave."

Yeah, it was tiring. His mother hit the nail on the head.

"I don't want to fight with him, Mom. I want him to accept me for me. I'm a bar owner. I'll always be a bar owner. What I will never be is a politician."

His mother nodded. "Eat your sandwich. You need your strength after a head injury, and you look way too pale to my liking."

Probably from the outdoor activity he got home from and the dismissal from the only woman he ever loved.

"I will, Mom."

Maybe. He didn't want to lie to her, but his appetite was still gone.

She smiled and turned around to leave. Right before she would've disappeared down the hallway, she stopped and looked at him.

"Chasity is a beautiful woman. One year, maybe my son might give me grandkids as a Christmas present."

Then she walked away with a beaming smile.

Well, shit.

Someone had seen them at Dragon Hill. The rumors were floating around, already hitting his mother's ears.

He pulled the plate closer to him. He needed to take care of his appetite. Because he had a big day ahead of him.

It was time to win Chasity's heart back.

He seriously needed a Christmas miracle.

UGH. Another day getting her workout in late. While she was happy she had managed to finish her workout, she liked to get it done at a certain time; otherwise, it threw her whole rhythm off for the day.

Look at how it turned out at Dragon Hill with Stu. What a disaster.

She let him kiss her. Thankfully, she had some self-control because as soon as he pulled away, she stopped the crazy impulse to pull him back in for another kiss. Because a little hill wouldn't stop her from devouring that man from head to toe.

He still had the ability to make her laugh. To show her fun and excitement, even after all these years.

He could still crush her heart and spirit with little effort as well.

He claimed he never told her she wasn't good enough. He had. Maybe he didn't say those direct words, but she heard them, nonetheless.

But whatever. She was over him. She would not allow anything to happen between them again.

Pulling into a parking spot in front of the Mulberry Diner, she wiped Stu from her mind. Or at least tried to. Once her shift started, it should be easier. She'd have her work to focus on.

Hopping out of her car, she dashed to the diner door and popped inside before an ounce of cold could sink into her skin. The temperatures were dipping lower as the day wore on, and that was saying something, as it had been brutally cold this morning.

"Hey, Chasity. How are you doing?" Theresa asked as she grabbed an empty plate and cup from the counter in front of her and transferred it to the counter behind her.

"I need a little pick-me-up before my shift. I didn't sleep well last night." Because that's what happened when a man she didn't want to think about penetrated her dreams. Such sweet, merry dreams she should not even dwell on for a moment.

"Sounds like you need a large to-go cup," Theresa replied with a knowing smile as if she understood what she was *not* saying.

Which put Chasity on high alert. Did Theresa know what happened between her and Stu? Or was she in so need of a jolt of caffeine she was seeing things that weren't there?

"A large cup would be great." Well, whatever Theresa might know, Chasity would ignore it.

She wasn't one for gossip anyway, especially if the gossip had to do with her.

Theresa nodded and turned around to the other counter where the coffeepot sat. She grabbed a large foam cup and poured the coffee to the rim. Chasity came in often enough where Theresa knew what she liked, so she added two scoops of sugar and a dollop of milk before placing a lid on the cup. Then she put a coffee sleeve over the cup and turned back toward her.

As she set the cup in front of her, another odd smile hit her lips. "Aiden stopped in for his daily coffee a little bit ago."

Chasity tilted her head in acknowledgment, unsure why Theresa was sharing that tidbit. It wasn't uncommon news.

She was married to Aiden and he always stopped in before his shift for a cup of coffee. Most people did, even though they knew Theresa made terrible coffee. A person got used to it after a while. Chasity sure did. She had developed a taste to the rancid flavor that she missed it when she made her own decent pot at home.

She laid a few bucks on the counter, not expecting change back, as she always insisted Theresa keep it for her tip.

"I don't know what I'd do without my coffee from you."

Theresa chuckled. "We both know it's terrible, but thank you."

She winked, then picked up her cup and took a sip. Yep. Strong and oh-so-disgusting, just the way she liked it. "Perfection. I don't know how you do it."

"Me neither." Theresa laughed again, then her expression fell. "I hate gossip, but I also hate being blindsided."

Oh, no. That didn't sound good.

"Aiden heard from Daphne—not sure where she heard it—that you were at Dragon Hill with Stu. Kissing and stuff."

And stuff?

What stuff?

Because she was all for more stuff, but once he pulled away, she resisted the temptation of more kissing so it didn't transform into any *stuff*.

This was bad news.

How in the world had they kept their summer fling a secret and now they couldn't even dive into a simple kiss without the entire town finding out? And they weren't even officially dating.

"It was a silly kiss. Nothing more. It's not a big deal.

We're not...it's not like we're...I mean, we aren't...there's nothing going on between us."

Wow. That sounded terrible. Like she word vomited complete nonsense.

Theresa looked sympathetic. "Sorry, I feel like I blindsided you when I was trying to help avoid that. It's none of my business what you two are or aren't. I hate how this town can shape things into something when people should just mind their own business." She rolled her eyes. "My brother comes to town for Christmas, Dusty has to stir shit up, and now some people think my brother is hanging out with him again and drinking and causing problems. It's frustrating how some people have to cause problems when there aren't any problems to begin with."

Yeah, Chasity had to agree. That was utter bullshit.

"I wasn't there when it happened, but I spoke to James that night. I know he wasn't causing problems with Dusty. He wanted nothing to do with him. I hope he's doing okay. That he's not letting this ruin his holiday."

"Erin can distract him quite easily, so he's doing okay," Theresa said with a gentle smile. "I didn't mean to upset you if I did. It wasn't my intention. It's been one of those days, you know."

Oh, she knew. She'd been having one of those days since the night she responded to a bar fight and came eye to eye with Stu after years of avoidance.

Chasity sat down on a stool, her eyes trailing to the counter as she rubbed a finger up and down the coffee cup. She had no idea why she felt compelled to tell Theresa anything, maybe because she brought up the subject first, but she knew she could trust her.

"Stu and I had a thing one summer years ago. Summer love. Whatever you want to call it. We're nothing now. I don't know why he kissed me today." One shoulder lifted and fell with despair.

Yet, a small weight that had held her down for such a long time fell off with that simple shrug. She felt a fraction lighter. It felt good.

"Because he wanted to. Men are complicated on occasion. Yet, they can be pretty simple to figure out. I think he's trying to tell you something without really telling you. Aiden kind of did the same thing with me before we started dating. Hence, why he kissed me under the mistletoe for the first time. Shocked us both."

Chasity raised her head, feeling a sort of strange bond with Theresa. Like she understood what she was going through with Stu. Her conflicted feelings. Her confusion. Her pull toward him when she shouldn't feel anything but disgust at the way he hurt her.

"I have no idea what to do, Theresa."

"Yeah, I know that feeling well." Theresa leaned forward and grabbed her hand, squeezing with comfort. "Ask yourself, what would make you happy? Because in the end, your happiness is what's important. And it's Christmas, so everyone should be happy."

Chasity couldn't help but smile. Theresa did love Christmas. As did Lynn, who always decked her bakery with Christmas galore. She always felt an extra merriness when she was around those two.

"Thanks, Theresa." Chasity stood up with her to-go mug in hand. "For the advice, and the heads up. I appreciate it."

"That's what friends are for." Then Theresa's eyes twinkled with merriment. "And if Stu is what makes you happy, make him work for it a little bit. Sometimes guys need that challenge."

"I'll keep that in mind."

Chasity headed for the door.

"Oh, and one more thing," Theresa said right before she would've stepped outside. "Get him to hang at least one Christmas thing in the bar. It drives me nuts he has no decorations up. Maybe a tiny tree or tinsel hanging or an ornament behind the counter. Something. Anything."

She laughed, suddenly having a splendid idea.

Oh, and Stu would put up a fight.

Perfect. Because she was gearing for one.

6

STU TRIED to keep the cheesy grin off his face when Lynn walked into the bar with a small white box wrapped with a big red bow around it.

"You are an angel." Stu laid two twenties on the bar and pulled the box closer to him when Lynn set it down.

She frowned in the adorable way she always did when she wanted to argue about money. He'd seen it a few times when she went back and forth with Elliot.

"You know I'm not taking all that. One twenty is even too much, and I didn't bring change with me."

He pushed the money closer to her side, refusing to lose this battle. "Lynn, you made a special delivery to the bar for me. Call it a delivery service. You deserve a tip. And it's Christmas. Merry Christmas."

He didn't always use the "Merry Christmas" sentiment, but sometimes it was called for.

She took one twenty and put it in her coat pocket. "I will not take both and that's final." Then she smiled. "But I won't argue about one. You're right. I did make a special trip here.

Be careful driving tonight. It's kind of sprinkling out right now. The roads are going to turn to ice soon."

Yeah, he had checked out the weather app a few times, keeping an eye on the weather. For a Wednesday night, he usually had more patrons than what he had right now, even for a generally slow day. Nasty weather always changed that. Which he was thankful for. He didn't want any accidents on his conscience.

"I appreciate this. I meant to stop before I headed to the bar, but I ran out of time."

Because he hadn't come up with any brilliant ideas in time. He wasn't even sure if this would be a great idea. Chasity wasn't likely to fall for just anything. Not that he was playing any sort of game here. He was trying to win her heart back. Too bad it took him fifteen years to figure out what he wanted in life.

Her.

Just her.

Lynn smiled warmly. "She'll like it."

He could feel his cheeks warm, embarrassed Lynn knew exactly what he was up to. Trying to woo Chasity.

Not that he was surprised. Officer Johnson had been making patrols and saw him kissing Chasity on the hill. Unfortunately, he then told Daphne, who spread the word in her kind, yet nosy way. One of the unpleasant joys of living in a small town. Nobody minded their own business.

"I hope so."

"Merry Christmas, Stu. I better get home to Eloise. She's been wanting me to do bedtime rather than Elliot." Lynn offered another pleasant, cheery smile then headed for the exit.

"Good night, Lynn. Drive safe." Then he waved to her.

He'd add an extra birthday present for Eloise when

February rolled around since Lynn made a special trip. Plus, Elliot and Lynn's almost two-year-old was too adorable. He always loved visiting them and playing with her. Hearing her sweet little words, especially how she said his name. Coming out sounding more like "two" rather than Stu.

Thinking of their wonderful family made him ache for his own family. Something he wanted one day. Shit. He wasn't getting any younger.

Grabbing the box, so tempted to open it, he put it in the small kitchen in the fridge so it would stay fresh. He had plans tonight. Or tomorrow. He hadn't quite decided yet. Chasity worked the night shift, as did he. He never closed his bar until one o'clock. He was pretty sure she got off her shift around eleven or so. He wasn't sure about the exact time, and without calling one of her coworkers to ask, making it obvious why he was, he'd have to guesstimate. But regardless, the bar closed after her shift, and she was probably asleep by the time he closed down. He was better off enacting his plan tomorrow.

Except he didn't want to wait. Being impulsive wouldn't help his case either. Such a fine line to walk and all he wanted to do was rush across it and take a leap of faith that she'd let him in—not only in her house, but her heart.

The evening dragged on. A few regulars popped in, had a few drinks, then left when the light sprinkles started to turn the roads to ice, as Lynn had predicted. Aiden had stopped in with a traffic report, suggesting he close up shop early so he didn't slide off the road himself.

He decided to take his own advice a little after eleven, another nice advantage to living in a small town—it wasn't unusual to close the bar on a whim. Also, a nice advantage being the owner of said bar. He had already sent his bartender, Chris, home an hour ago, considering it wasn't busy enough for them both to stay.

He lived on the outskirts of town, not too far from Aiden. Living outside of town made things more peaceful, which he coveted. Life was never peaceful growing up, especially with his father on the city council, and then making his way to the mayor's office. People in and out of the house. Parties that bored him to death. Pressure to be someone he didn't want to be. Yeah, he liked living outside of town, in his own space, in his own little world.

Another great advantage of living in a small town was he knew where Chasity lived. In a small apartment building not far off Main Street. As he closed up the bar, with the white box wrapped with a big red bow under his arm, he wondered whether it was wise to stop by her place before heading home. It's not as if he was in any extra danger as her place was on the way to his own house. He didn't have to go out of his way.

But would she open the door to him? What would she say?

Honestly, he wanted some answers. Like, why she thought he said she wasn't good enough for him. Because— lies. He never once said that. He never once thought that of her. If anything, he wasn't good enough for her.

Yep. He wanted answers today, not tomorrow. He found a parking spot and jaunted to her building with the box tucked underneath his arm. He knew she lived in the small apartment complex, but not exactly which apartment, so he had to trail down the list posted on the wall until he found her name.

Apartment number three. First floor. End of the hallway. The walk was short, yet each step felt like he wore hundred-pound weights. He was terrified of her reaction, of her possible rejection.

Probably what she felt like all those years ago. Rejection. And yeah, he wouldn't deny he had done that to her.

Not that he had wanted to.

He stopped in front of her door, his heart pounding like it could jump out of his chest at any moment.

How could he explain why he pushed her away? Why he'd let go of the one thing he never wanted to—and lived fifteen years without?

Because the more he thought about it, the more it sounded stupid in his head. He acted like a jackass of great proportions and now it was time to make things right.

He let his fear rule him. Never, ever again.

He knocked on the door. A bit hesitant, but loud enough where she should've heard. A few seconds—very long seconds—later, the door swung open.

Her hair looked like she had taken it out of a ponytail; it had an odd wave to it in the middle portion. Her beautiful blue eyes looked dull, not brimming with vibrancy and spirit, and ringed with dark shadows as if she'd had a rough day. Partly because of him? God, he hoped his actions earlier today hadn't put this desolate look on her face.

"Hi." The greeting came out more tentative than he liked, but he felt on very unfamiliar territory right now.

She leaned against the doorjamb, sighing. "What are you doing here, Stu?"

"A peace offering?" He lifted the white box with the bright red bow wrapped around it, adding in a smile that he hoped would gain him entry. "Please. Let me in...for a moment."

The please came out with a pleading ache in each syllable. He wanted entry. And he wanted to tell her how much he never meant to hurt her.

He wanted one more chance. A chance he didn't deserve but wanted, nonetheless.

———

CHASITY WANTED to scream in frustration.

Let me in...for a moment.

The dumb man. Didn't he know she had already let him in for over an entire decade? She was currently trying to purge him from her heart. This constant seeing him the last few days was not helping her.

But she also couldn't ignore the desperation in his tone or the want in her own bones.

"For a moment." Then she walked away from the door and headed to her living room. Her glass of wine sat next to the bottle she had grabbed to relax after a long, stressful day of work.

Her Christmas tree was lit up in front of her living room window. Ornaments scattered here and there. Some Santas and reindeers and silly looking elves. Some snowflakes and winter wonderland scenes. Some simple glittered gold bulbs that added a touch of magic to the branches. And, of course, bright colorful lights that always made her smile when she gazed upon it. Right now it was hard to conjure that smile. Especially with Stu's sudden arrival. What did he want?

Stu shut the door and followed her. When she took a seat on the couch, she saw him waging a war with himself. His eyes jogged back and forth between her small oval chair in the corner and the spot next to her on the couch. The spot next to her won the battle.

Her entire body sizzled with awareness as he sat down,

his thigh brushing her knee. When his decision won, he apparently was going all in. Touching her and everything. She wasn't sure she could continue to resist him.

"For you."

She eyed the white box, knowing exactly where it came from. Lynn was known for wrapping her treats with big red bows. Chasity always kept the ribbon because it felt wrong to throw it away. She had a whole closet full of them. She didn't know what to do with them, but she knew she couldn't throw it away. It almost felt like she was throwing away a part of Christmas or something, and she could never do that.

When his eyes pleaded with her to take the box, she gave up her internal war and took it from him. Carefully removing the bow—because of course, she was keeping this one too; the most special bow since it had come from Stu—she set it on the coffee table in front of her. Then she opened the box and started to laugh.

Four delicious round doughnuts sat inside, each decorated differently. One had green icing with colorful dots, mimicking a wreath with bright colorful lights lit up. Just like her tree. Had he known she liked colored lights over white lights? One had red and white icing stripes, making a pattern by alternating every other, reminding her of a candy cane. One had brown icing with one large dot of red, making her think of Rudolph. The last doughnut was glazed with white sprinkles all over it, which gave her the impression of snowflakes. All Christmas themed. Which surprised her and made her wonder, why Christmas? He didn't have one little decoration up in his bar, making her think he didn't enjoy the holiday.

The sweet, decadent smell drifted toward her nose. Oh, Lynn was a goddess at baking.

"They look and smell delicious." She tilted her eyes toward him. "But why? The sledding was a tie."

"I upset you earlier today, and I'm sorry. Like I said, it's a peace offering."

Stu scooted closer as if he could get any closer without touching her. His thigh rubbed against her leg. Then he grabbed the box and set it on the coffee table. Before she could protest, he took ahold of her hands, squeezing, as if sensing she wanted to pull away. She did. She wanted to push him away and demand he leave. Another part of her wanted to pull him closer and beg him never to let go. She hated her wishy-washy feelings.

"You said I told you you weren't good enough for me. I never said that. It guts me that you even think I think that. Because I don't." His head fell, yet his grip on her hands remained strong. "You know my dad's the mayor. We don't get along. He tries, even to this day, to mold me into a replica of him, and I hate it. I despise everything about him." He lifted his gaze and met hers, the pain doused in his eyes. "It's not a good enough excuse, but he's always tainted everything in my life, and I never wanted him to hurt you."

Chasity had to agree. It wasn't a good enough excuse. But, she could understand why back then he had pushed her away, unsure of how to fight his father. She wasn't a fan of the mayor. Not that she had much interaction with him, but the few times she had, she always got a slimy, icky feeling from him. Like he was acting playing nice. A little too much charm. A little too much politeness. She always felt bad inside for feeling that way since he was Stu's father. She had no idea Stu felt the same way about him. Her sister Hope, who worked for the man, wasn't a fan of him either. So interesting that the town didn't see the mayor for who he truly was.

Or maybe they did and chose to keep their thoughts to themselves. But not much gossip ever circled about the mayor.

Her feelings were so conflicted. She had no idea what to think. What was he saying? Why was he telling her all of this?

"I don't—"

"Wait," Stu said, cutting her off. But then he didn't add anything else.

What was she waiting for? A tiny grin appeared as she waited for him to continue, yet he looked like a deer stuck in headlights.

The longer they stared at each other, the more her grin spread, which produced a small smile from him.

Then he laughed. "I don't know why I cut you off. I guess I'm afraid to hear you ask me to leave." He leaned even closer, his mouth a few inches from hers. "I don't want you to ask me to leave."

"What do you want, Stu? This is all very confusing. For fifteen years, we ignored each other. And now..." Her eyes glided to his mouth, then back to his golden, hazel eyes that shimmered with a desire she felt deep in her bones. "And now it feels like we never stopped all those years ago."

"I want you. I want to make up for lost time. I want to show you how sorry I am for acting like an idiot. I want to feel like there's more to life than running the bar. I want another shot with you."

Then his lips touched hers. The kiss was light and care-free, yet she felt the unleashed power vibrating behind the touch. This could turn into molten desire and heat up her apartment in seconds if she let it.

She squeezed his hands, pressed her lips more firmly to

his, but then backed away, missing the loss of his soft touch immediately.

Theresa was right. She had to challenge him a bit. While she wanted to do more than kiss, she couldn't.

"Thank you for the doughnuts."

His expression fell from happiness into sorrow in one smooth move.

"You're welcome."

She bumped shoulders with him. "Don't look like your puppy just peed all over the floor. I didn't ask you to leave. Want a glass of wine and watch a movie?"

His eyes lit up like a Christmas tree sparking to life for the first time. Bright and merry and full of spirit. "I'd love that."

"Me, too."

She really loved it. She only hoped she wasn't setting herself up for another round of heartache. Because this was how it started all those years ago. He was all in...until he wasn't.

7

Rolling over, he groaned. Outstretching his hand, he met nothing but blankets and coldness. Not that he expected anything different, but in his mind, he imagined Chasity lying next to him. Of course, that wouldn't be possible either, unless she had come home with him last night, because he was in his own bed. So, his mind switched tactics and pictured himself lying next to Chasity in her bed. Much better.

Although, it's not as if he had expected to have sex last night when he stopped over at her house. He had simply wanted to apologize and find some common ground with her. Show her he was ready for a relationship this time. Win her heart back somehow. Sex would've just been an added bonus. But he understood why she had stopped him. He'd have to work for her affections.

Mission accepted.

Stu sat up and looked around his room—the sun peeking through the curtain, the clothes haphazardly tossed around the floor. He'd have to pick up in case she came over. He tended to be a bit on the messier side, but he didn't need to showcase that loud and clear. By the looks of her apartment last night, she was neater than him. That's okay. He could try harder to clean up. He could be better.

Then his eyes glided to his clock on the nightstand.

8:31 a.m.

Sometimes he could sleep in later, especially working until closing time at the bar. Sometimes his body woke him up way too early. Today was one of those days, but he wasn't mad. He had things to do.

The woman of his dreams to impress.

Jumping out of bed, he grabbed a clean set of clothes and headed to the bathroom. He took a quick shower and brushed his teeth in record time—for him, at least. He always took his time; he never had a reason to rush. When he should pick up the pace—like the horrible times he had to meet his father—he went slow on purpose.

Eating a small bowl of cereal and consuming a large glass of orange juice, he was almost ready to leave. He grabbed his running shoes and put them on, stretching his legs some. Then he grabbed his phone and house keys, tossed them into his jacket pocket, and headed out the door.

He drove into town and parked his car near her apartment when he saw Chasity jaunt out of the front door to her building and start jogging at a steady pace.

Shit. Now he'd have to run hard to catch up.

But not too hard.

He caught up to her in short order, his breathing a little heavier than he was used to. He worked out. Usually some weights and a few strengthening exercises, but he didn't generally run. Chasity ran without labored breathing. To be fair, though, he had to run faster to catch up to her.

Who was he kidding? She was going to kill him in this running business.

She cocked a tiny, adorable grin, but kept her steady pace. "Good morning, Stu."

"Morning."

His breathing started to level out as he caught on to her fluid pace.

"What are you doing?"

His arms swung in rhythm, the cold air brushing across his face in a soothing manner, rather than with brutality. Because it was cold as shit outside.

"I'm running. What are you doing?"

Sweet, beautiful laughter filled the chilly air. Oh, man, what he wouldn't do to hear that wondrous sound every day for the rest of his life.

Wow.

How come he never saw this before? How come it took a knock to the head with a barstool to realize Chasity was who he wanted to spend his life with? Who he always had wanted to spend his life with. He was just too scared to see it. So damn fearful.

"Why are you running? I've never seen you run before." Her pace slowed down a tiny fraction. "How did you know to find me out running?"

All in, baby.

Yep. He was all in.

"Well, not that I know your running schedule or anything, or keep tabs on you." Hell, no. He tried his hardest to avoid seeing her around town. That didn't mean it always worked. Plus, it was a small town. "But I know you always run on Thursday and Monday mornings at nine o'clock. So, I decided I was going to run at those times, too."

"Oh, you just decided that?" She shook her head as more laughter came out. More like, irritated laughter than the lighthearted kind from before.

"Yep."

Chasity picked up the pace.

Stu was forced to follow her lead.

"Keep up, old man." Then she took off at a sprint.

Shit.

She was honestly going to kill him. He'd have a heart attack before this run was completed.

But old man? He wasn't that much older than her. Only by a few months.

They ran all through Main Street. Then down a few blocks in a quiet neighborhood, turned around, and ran back through Main Street until they came back to her apartment.

By that time, he was breathing so heavily, his chest felt like it was going to burst open. He felt a small cramp in his right knee, the pain slight, but kind of spreading up into his thigh. His head pounded lightly. Not a full-blown headache, but a potential irritant if he didn't take some pain medication and make it go away. Who knew running would be so hard on his body?

"You look terrible," Chasity said with a quick toss of her head back and forth, then gestured for him to follow her.

He obeyed like a dutiful puppet to its master.

When they walked into her apartment, they headed for the kitchen where Chasity pulled out a pitcher of water from the fridge. After grabbing two large glasses from the cupboard opposite the fridge, she filled each glass up to the rim. He took off his jacket and tossed it over a chair in the dining room.

He rested against the counter on one side of the kitchen while Chasity stood on the other side and inhaled his entire glass.

"I'm impressed." Then her eyes softened. "I'm sorry. How

do you feel? You shouldn't have pushed yourself like that, especially since you don't run as often as I do. And your head. How is your head feeling?"

"My knee is a bit sore, but nothing I can't handle." He hated to admit it, but he never wanted to lie to her. Not ever again. "My head hurts a bit."

Her eyes shattered in remorse. "Oh, no, Stu. Why didn't you tell me? I would've slowed down."

Then she crossed the room and cradled his head in her hands as if she could soothe his pain away. He still felt the pounding, but her tender touch blocked it out just a little. He focused more on her touch rather than the pain.

"It's not a ton of pain. Nothing I can't handle." His hands found her waist and he pulled her closer. "I wanted to run with you. I had fun."

Her hands smoothed through his hair and down to rest on his shoulders. "So, does that mean I have a new running partner?"

He tossed his head back and forth as if contemplating that question when he knew the answer to it.

"Yeah, if it doesn't bother you."

"And if it bothers me?"

He grinned. "Then you're going to get annoyed with me real quick."

All in. Which meant he could not let anything hold him back, not even Chasity herself. He was bound and determined to show her what she meant to him.

"I need a shower."

Shit. He needed another one, too.

"Yeah, me, too."

He kissed her lightly on the lips as if silently asking if they could take that shower together. She kissed him back, bringing the kiss deeper, which had his heart soaring and his chances looking good.

Then she pulled back and smiled. A very mischievous smile that told him his chances were wrong.

"Do you want to meet at Mulberry Diner for a late breakfast?"

Fifteen years ago, they had hidden their relationship. More so because he had asked to keep it a secret. Because he hadn't wanted his father to intervene and ruin everything. Turned out, he ruined it all on his own.

Despite the rumors that they were seen at Dragon Hill kissing, going to Mulberry Diner in the middle of town would speak volumes. It would announce to everyone the rumors held merit.

And he was totally okay with that.

Because he wanted that Christmas miracle so badly. He had penned a letter to Santa in his head several times already. Maybe the big guy in red was real. It couldn't hurt to believe just a little.

"Brunch sounds great."

She narrowed her eyes as if wanting to chastise him for calling it brunch instead of a late breakfast. Then a beautiful smile lit up her face right before she kissed him breathless.

Damn.

If only she'd allow that shower together.

It didn't matter, though. She was in his arms, and he'd do anything to keep it that way.

CHASITY WONDERED what in the world she was doing as she walked into the diner, waved to Theresa who was helping another couple, and took a seat in a booth. Her sister Hope had called, but she missed it while in the shower, and she didn't want to be late meeting Stu. She'd call her back later today.

As she picked up the menu, although already had an inkling what she wanted, she knew why she was doing this. Because she needed to see if they could make a go of whatever was between them. She was sick of skimming by in life with okay guys who never reached the level of glorious intensity as Stu had. She didn't like comparing one guy to the next, but she couldn't help herself. Stu made her feel alive and like she was the queen to his kingdom.

Theresa wandered to her table after grabbing the coffeepot first. Chasity tipped over the empty coffee mug sitting on her table and smiled as Theresa started to fill her cup.

"Good morning. How was your run?" The twinkle in Theresa's eyes said she saw her run by earlier—with Stu by her side.

"Very nice. Stu will be joining me." She couldn't keep the giddiness out of her tone. It's like she was thrust back into high school, giggling about boys with her besties.

Most of her high school friends had skipped town the moment they could. Not everyone liked the small-town life. While she enjoyed her time away when she went to college, she liked Mulberry. Sure, gossip could be annoying, but she could live with it. Theresa wasn't a gossiper anyway, so she knew if she told her stuff, she'd keep it to herself. Funny, how comfortable she felt with Theresa. But over the years, coming in for coffee, and small events held around town, they had become friendly. Although they had never actually hung out outside of these types of things, she'd call Theresa her friend. It's too bad she was older than Theresa. It would've been nice to be friends in high school and have grown up into adulthood together.

"He looked like he was struggling at the end there," Theresa replied with a chuckle.

Her smile broadened as she lifted her coffee for a sip. "Yeah, he's not used to running. He will, though. He said he enjoyed it."

"Well, he's usually very prompt about things, so I'll fill up his cup now." Then Theresa flipped Stu's mug upright and poured him a steaming cup of coffee that didn't taste too bad.

As soon as Theresa walked away to help another patron, the door opened and Stu walked inside. His dark brown hair looked wet still and his cheeks were a rosy red. The wind wasn't brutal today, but it seemed to be picking up speed as the day wore on. Thank goodness they got their run out of the way.

Stu leaned down and planted a kiss to her lips before taking his seat across from her. Her hands trembled, the hot murky liquid swishing inside the cup as she stared at him.

Talk about announcing quite clearly what was developing between them. She wasn't sure how to feel about it.

Until his eyes sparkled with a desire that looked ready to be unleashed with one tiny word from her.

"How's the coffee today?" Stu asked as if he didn't shift her entire world off its axis with one simple kiss.

But she could pretend as if nothing monumental happened either.

"Not bad, actually."

Stu gave her a dubious look, then took a sip of coffee, only wincing slightly. "Hmmm, I'd have to agree."

They both laughed. Theresa came back over to the table a few short seconds later and took their order. Chasity ordered French toast with scrambled eggs and two slices of bacon. Stu ordered a ham sandwich with French fries—honey mustard on the side.

"So, do you work today?"

She shook her head. One of her rare days off getting so close to Christmas. She didn't mind working the holidays, letting others spend the time with their loved ones. Her dad moved out of town over ten years ago, even before her mom died. This year, though, she had Christmas off. She'd spend it with a nice lunch with her grandpa and Hope at the retirement center. She and Hope planned to have a quiet supper at her house, drinking wine, talking, gossiping, and reminiscing about their mom. She also planned to talk to her sister about Stu. It was time. Hope was two years younger than her, a little more free with her dating. But she knew Hope would understand and hopefully give her good advice on how to proceed with Stu. Although, it appeared they were proceeding with a relationship of some sort. If his kiss in public had any say about it.

"Do you?"

Stu half grinned, half grimaced. "Sort of, but I know the owner. I could ask for some time off."

Chasity laughed. Oh, how she had missed this. Missed him and the easy way he could always make her laugh.

But she had a better idea.

"What time do you have to be at the bar?"

"Chris is opening it up today. I was thinking of heading there around four or so. But I—"

"I have a surprise for you," Chasity cut in, unable to hold back a beaming smile. "I'll meet you at the bar later today."

Stu leaned forward, resting his elbows on the table. "Do I get a hint about this surprise?"

"Nope," she replied, popping the 'p' with emphasis.

He reached across the table and grabbed one of her hands, lightly brushing his thumb across her fingers.

"I swear I'm not going to screw up this time. I've missed you."

"I've missed you, too."

That was not easy for her to admit. Opening up to him, sharing her deep feelings, the emotions she held tucked inside for so long was so, so hard to let go.

"Well, well, well. What is this bucket of sunshine I see?"

Chasity cringed. Stu groaned.

Then he released her hand and twisted in his seat to see Dusty walking closer and stopping at their table. Chasity could smell a strong odor of alcohol emanating off him. The idiot was already drunk.

She glanced behind her shoulder, widening her eyes at Theresa, who nodded, understanding she should call the police. Luckily, the station was only a few buildings down from the diner.

"Can I help you with something, Dusty?" Stu asked as if he were inquiring about the weather and if it was going to snow out today. But she saw the tension in the way he clenched his jaw. In the way his eyes narrowed.

Oh, boy, she hoped Dusty didn't do anything stupid. Stu had a recent head injury, and he couldn't afford another one. Although he wasn't experiencing any bad signs from his last one, head injuries could be so tricky.

"You're a piece of shit. Why would I want your help with anything?" Then Dusty spit in his direction, his aim thankfully off as it hit the table near his coffee mug but not on Stu. "I got arrested because of you!"

Stu scooted back as Dusty started to lean forward. Before he could follow through with anything physical against Stu, Chief Duncan suddenly appeared from behind and grabbed him.

"Let's not do this, Dusty. You're on bail and waiting for your parole hearing violation. We don't want to add anything to it, now, do we?"

"I didn't do anything." He shoved the chief off, snarling the words at him.

Chasity didn't see the original altercation at the bar, but she could tell by Dusty's words he honestly believed he didn't do anything wrong. Oh, the things alcohol could make you believe. The stitches in Stu's forehead told a completely different story.

"Leave now, on your own, or you're leaving with me in handcuffs." Chief Duncan braced his stance, preparing for Dusty to make a move he wouldn't like. "Let's not do this, Dusty. Not so close to Christmas."

"Screw you!" Dusty hollered, slurring.

He moved like a cheetah, swiping Stu's coffee cup from the table and hurled it at the chief. Elliot ducked in time to avoid the hot liquid hitting him directly in the face. It hadn't been sitting that long to have cooled down much.

Dusty then went at Chief Duncan with both fists at the ready. Stu didn't hesitate. He vaulted out of his side of the booth and tried to grab Dusty from behind while Chief Duncan defended himself from the front.

Chasity didn't know what to do, so she stared at the mayhem unfolding before her. But Dusty was drunk, his reflexes slower than if he had been sound of mind. Chief Duncan, with help from Stu and Officer Stockman—who had arrived during the melee—was able to subdue Dusty, cuff him, and haul him out of the diner. Officer Stockman escorted him out.

Chief Duncan took a seat on a stool in front of the

counter, breathing heavily. Stu stood next to him, breathing heavily himself.

"You okay, Elliot? Did you get burned anywhere?" Stu asked.

Chasity took that as her cue to exit the booth. She didn't have any of her equipment on her, but that didn't mean she couldn't be of assistance.

"You ducked fast, but did any of the coffee hit your neck or skin?" she asked, not touching the chief, but tempted to do a thorough look.

Chief Duncan shook his head. "No, I don't feel any pain around my neck. Most of it hit my back. He kind of sucker punched me in the jaw, so that hurts." Then he chuckled. "But I'll be fine, Chasity. Thank you."

"He needs some serious help," Stu muttered as he took a seat next to the chief.

"Yeah, he does, except he won't get any. Some people can't see they need help." Chief Duncan shook his head, then looked around the diner. "Sorry about that, folks. Please enjoy the rest of your day. He won't be causing any more problems."

"I hope that means he won't be getting bail this time," Stu said softly, so only she, Chief Duncan, and Theresa—who stood near them—could hear.

The chief shrugged. "It's up to the judge. I imagine it won't be pretty when he sees him for his bail hearing." Then he stood up. "I better go home and change. Try not to let this ruin your day."

"You either, Chief," Chasity replied with a smile. There was no way she'd let Dusty ruin her day.

She had plans tonight with a man she hoped she had an actual future with this time.

The chief left. Theresa went to grab supplies to clean up

the mess Dusty created. She tried to help by grabbing napkins and wiping up the drips she could see on the counter and tables.

Once everything was picked up and everything restored to order, she and Stu reclaimed their seats and their food was placed in front of them. In all the chaos that had ensued, Bonzo hadn't stopped cooking.

When she had consumed her last bite, she leaned back and smiled. "So, we're still on for tonight?"

"Oh, yes." The heated desire flickering in his gaze said she'd be doing more than the surprise she had in store for him.

A lot more.

8

FOR A THURSDAY NIGHT, it wasn't as busy as he had anticipated. About twenty people were in the bar. Two sat at the bar, eight were playing pool in the corner, and the rest scattered in their own little corner, conversing with each other. Although, the roads were icy again. The weather was having fun messing with everyone. Instead of getting it over with and dumping hoards of snow on them, it decided alternating light rain and snow would be more fun. At night, when the temperatures dipped down, made the roads almost unbearable. Although the plows were always good about keeping the roads salted and as safe as they could make them.

Of course, Christmas was only a few days away, too. Everyone always celebrated it on different days, due to work or life commitments.

Either way, he didn't mind it not being packed—or too busy he couldn't handle juggling his time with customers and Chasity, who had yet to show up.

He could feel his phone burning a hole in his pocket.

Itching to pull it out and call her. Tell her to stay home, be safe.

Yet, he didn't because he wanted to see her. How selfish was that? Totally selfish.

After glancing at the clock, noting it was a little past six o'clock, and the roads were already becoming a mess, he knew he couldn't be *that* kind of a jackass.

Shit.

They never set an exact time she'd show up at the bar. Maybe she had gotten into an accident. Maybe that's why she wasn't here yet. Because he swore when she asked what time he would arrive that she had planned to arrive at the same time, too. The roads hadn't given him any problems. But Elliot had stopped in about twenty minutes ago, mentioning how the roads were faring, and a brief update on Dusty.

He saw the judge. Fifty-thousand dollar bail this time, unlike the twenty-five thousand he received a few days ago for the bar fight. Elliot didn't think he'd find a bail bondsman this time to bail him out. He'd be sitting until his parole violation hearing in three weeks. Stu tried to find an ounce of remorse for the guy, but he couldn't manage it. Not when he touched his forehead and felt the few stitches gracing his face. Dusty needed help. And if he wasn't going to get it on his own, he'd pay the consequences another way.

Stu thought about asking whether Elliot relayed any of this info to Chasity, but he didn't dare voice it. Plus, he was friends with Elliot. He came to him out of courtesy and their friendship to give him an update. He knew Elliot was friendly with everyone—being the chief of police kind of required that of him—but he wouldn't say he and Chasity were friends. So, he figured, in the end, Elliot hadn't reached out to her.

Odd and surprising thing, too. Nobody had asked him about Chasity and what was going on. Not even Elliot. Although he had looked preoccupied. Probably had to do with Eloise. He had seen Lynn earlier when he left the diner and she seemed worried, leaving her shop early because Eloise came down with a fever. Hopefully, it turned out to be a small bug and her fever broke soon. He hated to see his friends stressed, especially concerning their children.

He glanced at the clock again. Another two minutes had gone by. He should call Chasity. Coming out tonight wasn't the best idea. They could hang out tomorrow before both their shifts.

Pulling out his phone, something he should've done fifteen minutes after Elliot left, he tried calling Chasity.

No answer.

His heart started to pound. Why wasn't she answering?

Well, she didn't have to answer his call. She didn't want to be bothered right now. They weren't dating officially or anything. She could've changed her mind about showing up. Maybe she decided she wanted nothing to do with him. He wouldn't blame her. He hurt her—unintentionally, and for reasons he thought were good, but hurt her, nonetheless.

He tried calling her again. No answer.

"Hey, Stu, can we get another round?" Rick, one of the guys playing pool, asked.

Stu pasted on a smile and tried to shake off the terrifying feeling that something bad had happened to Chasity. She was ignoring his calls. That's all. He shouldn't worry about anything.

"Yeah, of course. It'll be right there." Stu nodded at Rick, who tapped the bar happily and sauntered back to the corner of the bar.

"I got this, boss," Marcy said from her end of the bar

where she stood talking to Bill and Larry, who came in most weekends for a few drinks.

Chris had switched shifts with Marcy. As long as his employees followed through with their agreement, he didn't mind when people switched shifts and whatnot. He trusted all of them.

Stu didn't have the energy to argue, especially with how worried he was about Chasity.

"Thanks, Marcy. If you need me, I'll be in the kitchen." Then he walked into the back, inhaling a few deep breaths.

She was okay. He had to believe she was okay. She was simply ignoring his calls.

Except, no matter how many times he repeated that in his mind, he couldn't seem to shake the eerie sensation that had his skin crawling with unease. Something bad happened.

He didn't know how long he stood there near the doorway to the kitchen, resting against the wall, inhaling and exhaling with large breaths. But that's how Marcy found him when she popped her head through the kitchen door.

"Hey, boss, you got a visitor."

He whipped his head at Marcy. "Who?"

Because he was not in the best mental frame right now to beat the bush with anyone. He could feel himself teetering on the edge of madness if he didn't hear Chasity's voice soon, just to know she was okay.

"Chasity."

Like that, all his worries deflated. A huge breath exhaled, then he nodded, to let Marcy know he heard. She looked at him quizzically but didn't press him for details on why he seemed so out of sorts. Because behavior like this was out of character for him. He was always cool, calm, and collected. He had to be, especially with drunks that thought they could do anything in their alcohol-induced minds.

He took a few more deep breaths, double-checked his phone to see if he missed a call from her, which he hadn't, then stepped out of the kitchen.

Chasity stood on the other side of the bar with an adorable smile on her face. Her hair looked windblown—Elliot had mentioned the wind had picked up speed, yet no snowstorm on the weather radar—and her cheeks were a rosy red.

A large brown box sat on the bar.

"Hey, you okay?" Her smile dipped.

He hadn't masked his concern as well as he thought he had. "I tried calling you. I was going to reschedule this. I heard the roads were getting bad."

Chasity chuckled. "I swear they've been bad all week. Sorry I was late. I was on the phone with my sister."

Yeah, he knew her sister. He had conversed with Hope in the last fifteen years more than he had with Chasity. How sad was that? Although, unlike Chasity, Hope ventured into his bar now and again and he didn't want to appear rude. But based on all his interactions with her, he didn't think she knew that he and Chasity had ever been an item.

"What's in the box?" He wasn't in the mood to get into any family dynamics. Because he knew Hope worked for his father. Talking about his father never made him feel good.

Chasity inhaled, then let it out as a wide smile appeared. "Now, I hope you don't get mad at me or anything, but this is happening."

That didn't sound good.

"What is happening?"

Her smile not only lit up her face, her lips widening, two

small dimples appearing, but her eyes sparkled with merriment. A bit mischievous intent as well.

She opened the lid to the box and pulled out a tiny
Christmas tree.

"We need to decorate the bar a little bit. We need some
Christmas cheer in here."

For a second there, she had him worried. But this? He
could handle this. Maybe.

"Are we now?"

"Yep," she replied, popping the 'p' with emphasis. Something he noticed she loved to do still to this day. He always
found it adorable that one summer long ago.

Especially when he had her right where he wanted her.
In his arms. Loving her body. Making her beg for more.
Please, Stu. Don't stop. Something she always said when he
would tease her if he should stop. She always pronounced
stop with a pop to the p. He loved it.

She must've seen the slight hesitation in his eyes,
although he maintained a fluid smile. But she leaned across
the bar, frowning.

"Is there a reason you don't like Christmas? I'm sorry if
I'm overstepping my boundaries here."

He leaned forward, resting his elbows on the bar, his
mouth close to her lips. Damn, he wanted to kiss her.

"I don't mind Christmas."

She bit her lip, her eyes trailing to his mouth, yet neither
made a move forward. "So, why no decorations? You're like
the only business in town with nothing up."

Not a conversation he wanted to have, but if he wanted
to make things work this time with her, he had to be honest
with her—about everything.

"My father uses the holiday as a gimmick. To reel people
into his way of thinking on any kind of matter. He uses it as

a political gain. I hate that. I don't hate the holiday. Six years ago, when my uncle passed, he left the bar to me. My dad's brother. They never got along. To spite my father, he never decorated the bar for Christmas. Oh, man, my father would harp on him about it all the time during the holidays." Stu almost dropped his gaze, hating to relive these memories, but he couldn't. He would let her see all the pain he ever endured by his father. Not that he wanted to, but he would, hoping she'd understand a little bit more of why he acted the way he had years ago.

"When the bar became mine, my father hounded me to sell. He wouldn't let up. It was a huge fight. It was the first year I never showed up for Christmas at their house, which I knew broke my mother's heart. But I was done. My uncle wasn't there anymore, and he made the holidays more bearable with his presence. I decided, in honor of my uncle, I wouldn't decorate the bar."

Chasity's eyes softened, the ache he felt mirrored in her eyes. As if she felt how much he hurt. Then she lifted a hand and brushed it across his cheek. The softness in her touch. The understanding meant more to him than she could ever know.

"I'm sorry. I had no idea."

He shrugged, placing a hand over hers, so she wouldn't pull away from him. He liked her touch.

"My father hides his evil well." A lame laugh escaped. "Evil is too strong of a word. But I don't have many happy memories of him."

"So, you like Christmas?" she asked tentatively, as if afraid to even ask him such an innocent question.

"I do. I don't dislike it. It's just another day to me, to be honest."

She leaned even more and broke the distance, pressing

her sweet lips to his. "We don't have to put any of this up. I didn't mean to hurt you in any way."

He lowered their hands, then wound his other hand behind her neck, pulling her in for another kiss. "You didn't hurt me. You did open my eyes, though. By not hanging anything up, I still feel like he has some sort of power over me, and I despise that. I guess it wouldn't hurt to hang a few things. What else is in that box?"

Her eyes lit up with giddiness as her lips spread wide, tilting upward. "Not a lot, but it's some fun stuff. You'll love it."

He kissed her one more time. Long, languid, and bestowing a promise there was more of that to come later. Tonight. He would have her tonight. If she'd have him.

"Let's do this."

Then he stood up straight, rolling his eyes when he caught sight of the guys in the corner making smoochie faces, teasing him.

Chasity noticed as well. "No hiding anything this time."

He squeezed her hand he had yet to let go of. "I'm never hiding anything ever again when it comes to you."

CHASITY HAD ARGUED with herself the entire time she drove to the bar. Stemming from an argument she had with her sister.

Was she doing the right thing trying to rekindle what she and Stu once had? Because according to Hope, she was making a colossal mistake. Hooking up with a Hafferty—in her sister's eyes—spelled disaster with a capital D. Hope said she would know since she worked for his father.

But based on the little Stu told her, he was nothing like

his father. He didn't even get along well with him. That didn't make Stu a bad guy. He hid his feelings well about his father because she hadn't heard many rumors that they didn't get along. Although, he never showed up to the annual Christmas party. That should've told her something. But she never went either.

"Well, let's get this decorating party started," she said, hoping to dispel the rest of the lingering bad vibes from her system.

She hated when she fought with her sister, and over something they should've never argued about. Hope had called her before she was about to leave. If she would've known Hope was calling her to warn her off from Stu after hearing the rumors flying around town, she never would've answered the phone.

Hope didn't know Stu. Not like she did. Which was comical, in a way. She didn't know Stu either. A summer fling over fifteen years ago didn't say she knew the man. Physically? Oh, yeah, in every possible way. Emotionally? Not so much. But she wanted to get to know him more. So, here she was.

"I won't cross the line with Christmas music. I'm not a fan of the music. It's overplayed on the radio."

She smiled, soaking up every bit of information he was willing to toss her way. She wanted to know everything about him. His secrets. His fears. His likes and dislikes. She wanted to know that what she felt all those years ago wasn't a fluke. That he was the man she wanted in her life for always.

Even though she enjoyed Christmas music, she wouldn't let this sway her feelings toward the do-not-date category.

"I can compromise." She picked up the small tree with a few strands of white lights. It was the only one left in the store when she stopped by. She would've preferred colored lights, but what could she do? She didn't have time to drive to another store. Flicking the switch on the bottom from off to on, her smile brightened when the lights lit up in all its merriness. White lights? Colored lights? She simply loved a lit Christmas tree.

Hopefully, Stu would remember to turn the lights on every day. It was only a few more days until Christmas, so it shouldn't be too hard for him. Since it was battery operated, she figured the batteries would hold that long.

"The tree would look nice by the cash register." She pointed behind him where the computerized machine sat, a few bottles of alcohol—the top-shelf kind—lined up behind it.

"Works for me. You're the expert." He grinned as he took the tree from her hand and positioned it by the register.

He stepped back a moment, eyeing the tree, moving it here and there until he found a spot he was satisfied with. She knew then, this wouldn't be hard at all.

She pulled the rest of the Christmas decorations out of the box. She offered a place for him to put it, where he usually agreed and hung it up.

Some silver tinsel hung against the wall under the first shelf where bottles of alcohol lined above it. Small ornaments were placed by the tinsel. Just a few. A reindeer. A snowman. Santa holding a bag full of toys.

Over by the front door, he hung mistletoe. He rolled his eyes at first when she pulled it out of the box, but then proceeded to grab a chair and hung it up. Then he refused to move from the spot until she joined him under the mistletoe where he kissed her breathless.

Each time his lips met hers, she wanted more. She

wanted to beg him not to stop. To devour her from head to toe. Remind her of his soft, tender touch.

From there, two other couples had fun standing under the mistletoe, kissing like they were gearing for a contest of who was the best kissing couple.

They all laughed, enjoying the festivities.

The last thing she pulled out of the box was a decal for the front door that read Merry Christmas. She positioned it at eye level when someone opened the door while Stu had hung the mistletoe.

When they were finished with the decorations, Stu poured her a glass of wine and grabbed himself a beer. She didn't argue when he stayed behind the bar while she took a seat on a stool. He was working, so she understood.

"Not so bad, uh?" she said with a light smile.

She didn't know how to proceed with the conversation. Because she sensed it probably wasn't as easy as he made it look, hanging the few decorations she brought. He had his reasons for no decorations. While some might think it silly, the reason was important to him. She would never make him do anything that he didn't want, but he hadn't seemed to mind. She was no expert, but it was probably good for him to do this. Like he said, not hanging anything was still giving his father control that he didn't wish to give.

"Yeah, it was painless. I enjoyed hanging the mistletoe," he said with a delicious smirk that spoke volumes.

Oh, that smirk said everything. That he was ready whenever she was ready. And she decided she was oh so ready. No more making him work for things. Giving him a challenge. Her body needed him as close as it could possibly get.

"Don't forget to turn the Christmas tree off and on from now until Christmas. It doesn't look as festive without the lights on."

"Work in progress here, I might fail," he said with an adorable chuckle that said he was teasing.

"Christmas is three days away. You can manage to do it for three days."

His eyes twinkled with mischief. "Maybe."

She took a sip of wine. He mimicked her actions by taking his own sip from his beer. She wouldn't say the moment turned awkward all of a sudden, but something in the air shifted. A sort of tension. Sexual tension.

Lots of sexual tension that would remain until they cleared the air altogether.

She didn't know if she could sit here until the bar closed, feeling the attraction grow between them and not be able to do anything about it. Like, have her dirty, wicked way with him.

Maybe they were moving too fast.

Maybe they weren't moving fast enough.

She hadn't had much to drink, but the few small sips she had were messing with her head. She needed air and some space.

Gulping down more of her wine, a few sips left sitting on the bottom, she stood and grabbed her jacket from the stool next to her.

"Leaving already?" His eyes filled with surprise and a touch of pain.

"I don't want to drink too much, not with the roads getting icy." She tried to twist her lips into a gentle smile, one he wouldn't misinterpret. She wasn't saying she was done with him altogether, but she needed a breather. "Drive safe tonight."

His brows dipped low as his lips fell downward. "I will." Then he leaned closer. "Did I say something wrong?"

She shook her head. "You're saying everything right."

He tilted his head, his brows slightly puckered low. "I still feel like I did something wrong here. Chasity—"

She pressed forward, slamming her lips to his, cutting off whatever he was about to say. The last thing she wanted to do was make him worry he was doing everything wrong. Since this morning when he joined her for her run, he had been doing everything so right.

She pulled back, sighing. "I need a bit of space right now. I can't explain why." Her eyes dropped to the counter, embarrassed by her wishy-washy feelings she couldn't help but display. What was wrong with her?

The only thing she could blame it on was her sister's phone call. Hope had planted some seeds of doubt in her mind that she should avoid anyone with the last name Hafferty. Her heart said screw it and to take a leap of faith. Her mind told her to take things slow and guard her precious heart.

A warm hand wound around her neck, pulling her closer. She lifted her gaze, seeing the same worrying confusion she felt mirrored in his eyes.

"One moment at a time. We can do this. I know I screwed things up years ago, but I'm trying here. Call me when you get home so I know you made it safely."

She nodded, meeting his lips when he moved closer. His tender touch always reminded her why she fell for him in the first place. He was so attentive to her needs, her feelings, her thoughts.

He let her go when she pulled away and put her jacket on. She grabbed her purse from the counter, then pulled her hat and scarf out of the pocket of her jacket and put them on.

"Seriously, call me when you get home," he reiterated, the concern flaming in his whiskey-colored eyes—tiny flecks of flames jumping up and down, enhancing the brightness of his eyes.

"Of course. I will." Then her lips moved upward. "Maybe...maybe you can stop by on your way home to see for yourself I made it safely."

His frown instantly turned upside down. His eyes sparkled with immense desire. "Definitely. If you're sure?"

"Honestly, Stu, at this point I'm so unsure about a lot of things. I want you, but I'm scared."

"The last thing I ever want to do is hurt you again. I won't hurt you again. I promise."

She was putting all her faith into that one huge promise.

"I'm holding you to that promise."

She just hoped she wasn't making the worst mistake of her life—having faith in his promise. Because her sister seemed to think the opposite, and she had yet to see her sister be wrong about anything.

9

HE'D MADE many mistakes in life, but hurting Chasity felt like the worst kind of mistake. He still needed to ask her why she thought he said she would never be good enough for him. After the way she retreated so quickly, one second enjoying herself, the next fleeing like he'd burned her with a hot poker, they needed to talk. Not the kind of talk they'd been having, but a serious talk about what happened so long ago. Although, he had already grazed the surface of it somewhat. But he needed to dig a little deeper and have a real talk with her.

When she called him telling him she got home okay, all he could think was he needed to be there. She had sounded fine. Like everything was good between them. But he needed to make sure they were good because the way she left the bar brought a strange frightening sensation in his gut.

They weren't fine. They could be though if they talked through it.

Calling Aiden, who he knew was on duty tonight, he

inquired about the roads. He hated worrying about people driving home after having a few drinks. While he shouldn't worry so much, he wasn't responsible for everyone and the decisions they made, he did. It was his bar. He served them the alcohol. So, it was his responsibility.

Aiden told him the roads were slightly slick but drivable. He informed him they weren't as bad as a few days ago. That made Stu feel better, but he still decided to close the bar up at midnight. Only five patrons were hanging around, and nobody whined about leaving early. They understood.

By the time he cleaned up and put everything in its place, with help from Marcy, it was a little past midnight. He locked up and waved goodbye to Marcy, making sure her car started and she was safely on her way before he even started his truck. Her car could be touch and go sometimes. He'd been telling her it was time for a new car, which she agreed. One of the reasons she picked up shifts was to save as much money as she could.

He took his time on the short drive from his bar to Chasity's place. Aiden hadn't lied. The roads weren't as bad. The light rain had switched to snow. They had a good crew who salted and sanded the roads often to keep the roads as passable as possible.

As he rounded the corner to the street to Chasity's apartment, he slowed down, eyeing the truck cockeyed in the road. It looked like Bentley's truck. The door was ajar, the lights blazing inside the cab. But he didn't see anyone in the truck.

Pulling over to the side, he shut off his truck, and jaunted outside, his heart pounding as he neared Bentley's truck. The inside cab was empty.

Well, shit. Where was he?

"Bentley!" Stu shouted, cupping his mouth.

Light drops of snow hit him as he circled the truck, checking out the area, trying to figure out where he disappeared.

"Bentley! Where are you?"

As he rounded Bentley's truck, he heard a low moan in the distance. The wind blew haphazardly around him, the snow pelting his face. Better than rain. He was grateful for that. But it made everything so much colder. He hadn't even put on a hat or gloves. Now that he thought about it, his hat and gloves were back at the bar in the kitchen area where they kept their belongings during a shift.

"Bentley!"

"Yo, Stu, over here."

Stu shifted his attention to a semi-dark alleyway a few feet away. Jogging in that direction, he had to slow down when he almost slipped and fell. The last thing he needed was another hit to the head or break a bone in his ass or something. He had a woman to love tonight. To show her in all ways possible how sorry he was.

The alley was dark, not much light filtering from the street. He went about ten feet before he came upon Bentley crouched low to the ground and a black muddy dog laying on its side.

"Shit. What happened?" Stu asked, crouching low next to him.

"I don't know, man. He came out of nowhere. I'm driving home from my shift, trying to be careful as the road is slick in some places, and he was suddenly in my path. I slammed on the brakes, felt a slight bump, and then a streak of black dash off this way. I must've hit him." Bentley looked at him with soulful eyes, the pain stretched in his entire expression.

"I'm afraid to pick him up. I don't see any bleeding, but he keeps moaning and won't move."

"I'll help you. First things first, let me call Jax and tell him to meet us at the clinic."

Bentley nodded. "Good idea. I'll go grab a blanket from my truck."

Stu rubbed the dog's head soothingly, the poor boy whimpering as he did. Then he pulled out his phone and roused Jax out of a good sleep, telling him to get his ass in gear and meet them at the clinic. With no blood in sight, Stu couldn't pinpoint what kind of injuries the dog had. Yet Bentley was sure he felt a bump with his truck. He most likely hit the poor dog and he had internal injuries they couldn't see.

Bentley came rushing back with a thick brown wool blanket. Not surprising he had a blanket in his truck. He probably also had other emergency supplies. Stu did. Always good to carry an extra set of warm clothes and a blanket in case of an emergency, especially in the winter.

He said a quick goodbye to Jax and then helped Bentley transfer the dog to the blanket. A small cry echoed in the chilly night air as they laid the dirty dog on the blanket. No collar. Filthy, tangled curly hair. Out on the streets with no one else in sight. Definitely a stray. And in this cold weather, Stu wasn't sure how the dog was surviving. In the dark, his thick, dirty fur made it appear as if he was well-fed, but he felt the bones and the frailness when he picked him up. He was malnourished.

Bentley gently scooped the dog up wrapped in the warm blanket and carried him back to his truck where he had kept the passenger side door open.

"I'll meet you at the clinic," Stu said as he walked back to his truck and Bentley rounded his own with quick precision.

He didn't own any pets, but that didn't mean he didn't like animals. Seeing one in pain was making his heart hurt. The poor mutt.

Jax was standing outside the vet clinic in a pair of flannel pants and a gray T-shirt, although he had thrown on his white lab coat, when they arrived.

"What happened?" Jax asked as they followed him inside. Bentley held the dog in his arms as they headed to one of the back rooms.

Bentley relayed everything he had told Stu. After unwrapping the blanket, Jax went to work examining the dog. In the bright lights compared to the dark alley, they could finally see the poor dog was bleeding. Most of his tangled fur was black with his feet and chest white. Mixed with dirt and mud near his hind legs was a murky red color that could only be considered blood.

"I'll have to take an x-ray, but his right leg is hurt for sure." Jax sighed. "The x-ray will tell me more."

"I tried to swerve, man," Bentley said in a whisper, the heartache bleeding in his voice.

"I know. It could be worse. He could already be dead." Jax smiled. "I'm going to take good care of him. I called Clara in to help me. You guys can go home and I'll let you know the prognosis. I don't see a collar on him."

"No one was around either. Can only assume he's a stray," Stu said.

"Either way, he'll be right as rain after I'm done with him," Jax said affectionately as he rubbed the dog's head. "Go on. You two go home and I'll update you tomorrow. I promise."

"I feel weird leaving," Bentley mumbled, his eyes filling up with tears.

"Yeah, well, I can't have you back here when I'm operating. If I have to, that is. It'll be fine, Bentley. It's not your fault. It could've happened to anyone," Jax said, trying to reassure him.

"Come on, man. We'll check on the little guy tomorrow. He's in good hands with Jax," Stu said. He didn't know what else to say or how to comfort him. Because Jax was right. It could've happened to anyone. He could've hit the dog. He was right behind Bentley. If he would've left a few minutes earlier, he'd be the one almost in tears because he hit a dog.

Bentley finally nodded and allowed Stu to push him out of the room. He glanced back at Jax, who nodded in thanks, then he got right to work helping the dog.

Stu knew he was in good hands. He was the best vet in the area. A lot of people not even from Mulberry brought their pets to Jax because they knew they'd be getting the best care. Not to mention, Jax had a heart of gold. It didn't matter if you didn't have enough money. The pet's health and safety were always his number one priority. Like now. Helping a stray. No owner. No one to pay the bill. Only a heartless person would let an animal die like that, and Jax was not that person.

"Can you make it home okay? I can drive you," Stu said as he walked with Bentley to his truck.

"I'll be fine. I'll be driving like a snail. I can't believe I hit him," Bentley said in almost a trance.

Stu worried whether he was going to be okay or not. But then Bentley shook his head as if shaking off all the bad vibes to have a clear head once he sat in his truck.

"I'll meet you here tomorrow morning," Stu said, knowing he'd be here checking on the dog whether Bentley would or not. But he knew Bentley would be here first thing when the clinic opened. As would he. Eight a.m. couldn't come soon enough.

Jax would send them a text with an update as soon as he knew more, though.

Bentley nodded and slid into his truck. Stu climbed into his truck and waited for Bentley to drive away first.

He had to backtrack the way he came to go to Chasity's apartment. Although his mood wasn't as happy as it had been when he left the bar, he had made a promise. He wouldn't hurt her again. So, he had to show up tonight.

Even though it was nearly two a.m., and she was probably sound asleep, he wouldn't hurt her like that.

A promise was a promise.

A LOUD KNOCK SOUNDED, jerking Chasity out of her sleep. She jerked a little too hard, tumbling from the couch to the floor, almost knocking her head on the edge of the coffee table. Groaning in despair and at her clumsiness, she hit the side of her phone sitting on the table to catch the time.

2:07 a.m.

Geez. Who was knocking on her door so late?

Standing, the sleep still heavy in her eyes, her mind trailed to the only person with enough nerve to show up this late.

Stu.

She had expected him a lot earlier. The bar closed at one. Therefore, he should've been here closer to one rather than two. Maybe something happened at the bar. Another incident, albeit without Dusty since he was still locked up on his latest charges.

Although, she couldn't be too upset at Stu for arriving so late because she had waited up for him, losing the battle with her eyes and fell asleep on the couch.

He said he'd stop by and he didn't go back on his word.

Wiping her eyes as she walked to the door, she shook her body, trying to get the cricks and cracks loose. Then she double-checked through the peephole to make sure it was Stu and opened the door once she confirmed her suspicions. It might be a small town, but living in the city for college taught her to be vigilant regardless of where she lived.

He looked tired and worn-out, like she felt.

"I'm sorry. You were sleeping, weren't you? I should've called," he said as he ran a hand through his hair.

She reached up and brushed a hand across his scruffy cheek. Growing a beard looked good on him. Shaved. No shaving—a look he donned when he was younger. The man was sexy either way. He leaned into her touch, closing his eyes.

"Did something happen?"

She could only assume something had otherwise why had it taken so long for him to show up. Unless he was already having second thoughts. She should've never put her heart on the line as she was doing.

His eyes gradually opened. "Yeah, I closed the bar early and should've been here a long time ago, but I ran into Bentley on the road. He—"

"Oh my gosh! Is he okay? Are you okay?" She pulled him inside the apartment and shut her door, wrapping her arms around him in the biggest hug she could.

She had seen the tiredness in his eyes the moment he opened the door, but she had no idea the situation could've been something like this. She had so many things to say to him still, so many things she had left unsaid and she almost lost her chance because of an accident that could've been much worse. She was too afraid to lift her head and ask him more about Bentley. Was he okay? How was Emma? Did they need to go to the hospital?

She felt him press his lips to the top of her head and exhale slowly.

That couldn't be good. Bad news was on the way.

"You didn't let me finish, Chasity. I didn't mean I literally ran into him. I mean, his truck was parked in the road and I found him in the alley where he accidentally hit a dog. I helped him take the poor thing to see Jax. He's fixing him up as we speak."

She lifted her head, grateful to hear Bentley was all right, but hurting inside that a dog got hit.

"He's going to be okay? The dog?"

Stu nodded. "At least, Jax said he would be. I hope so. I'll check it out tomorrow. He was dirty and alone, definitely a stray. Poor thing. Bentley took it hard. He feels terrible he hit the little guy."

"Of course. I'm sure he didn't mean to. It was an accident like you said. Come on. You're cold." Then she pulled him toward her living room where she snuggled under her blanket and waited for him to take off his coat and join her.

She wrapped it around them as soon as he sat down and rested her head against his chest.

"You okay?"

He wound his arm around her, squeezing her closer. "I'm much better now. I know it's late. I don't have to stay long."

"How are the roads? They weren't too bad when I left." She didn't want him to leave.

Who was she kidding? She asked him to stop by for one reason. To have sex. Since he was here, leaving was the last thing she wanted. Although, Stu probably wasn't in the mood, nor was she after the news he imparted her with. But she still didn't want him to leave. She wanted him to stay. Hold her in his arms, knowing he was real and back in her life. That things between them could be more than just physical. Because fifteen years ago, while they had ventured off to a few places to have fun and talk, most of the time they spent together had been between the sheets—figuratively speaking, as they never actually made it to a real bed. She wanted more than sex. She wanted it all. His heart and soul. His dreams and fears. His goals. His tragedies in life. His triumphs. All of it.

Sex would just be an added bonus.

"They're okay. Drivable. Bentley swerved some slamming on the brakes, which helped him not hit the dog head-on."

She hugged him tighter, hating the sadness in his tone.

"Stay."

She let out a long, slow breath as she waited for his answer. She didn't have to wait long.

"Okay."

"I'm tired, and I imagine you are, too. Let's go to bed." She waited for him to agree, then stood up first, holding out her hand.

"Do you mind if I grab a quick shower first? I feel..." Stu haphazardly lifted a shoulder. "Dirty or something."

"Of course."

She grabbed him a towel from the hallway closet and then headed to her bedroom where she curled up and fell asleep, even though she tried to keep her eyes open. She wasn't used to staying up so late. She normally crashed when she got off a shift.

The bed shifted some time later, she wasn't sure when, waking her up. Stu scooted closer, pulling her into his arms.

She had on a long T-shirt pajama set, but she felt right away all he had on before he climbed into bed was his boxers.

While that could be tempting, she was too tired to do anything but hold him and close her eyes once again.

The last thing she thought she heard before she drifted off to sleep once more was, "I swear I won't screw this up again, Chasity. I'll prove to you how much I love you."

10

Stu woke up, stretching out his hand, and met coldness.

Damn. It had all been a dream. A very, sweet heavenly dream that he wanted to replicate every day of his life. Falling asleep next to Chasity, holding her in his arms, was a dream come true. But a dream only.

Life sucked.

And he could only blame himself.

He must've been so tired last night driving home from the clinic, he thought he stopped at Chasity's place instead of driving home.

He opened his eyes, hating to get up, but knowing he had a busy day ahead of him. Then he gradually looked around the very unfamiliar room.

White walls—unlike his light blue walls—were decorated with different pictures of the ocean. Waves crashing on the beach. Seashells dotted along the shore. A dolphin peeking out of the water close to the shore.

Wow. It hadn't been a dream after all. He was in Chasity's room, except she wasn't with him.

His spirits lifted, but not completely. Because in a perfect world she would've still been in bed next to him.

They both had been exhausted last night. Sex or anything else had been the furthest thing from his mind. He had just wanted to wash off the gruesomeness of the night, fall into bed, and hold her tight. Shit. He hadn't even kissed her as he mentally retraced last night.

What a moron.

He had even whispered he loved her when he felt her body relax and her eyes shut. He knew she didn't hear him, and he didn't want her to. But it felt good to get it out. To finally say it out loud—with her in the vicinity.

He needed to tread carefully. Letting her know how he felt at the start of their tentative relationship wouldn't be wise. He was already skating on thin ice with her. One wrong move and she'd shove him out of her life.

He couldn't let that happen.

Getting out of bed, he looked around the room for his clothes, realizing he left them in the bathroom. Well, they slept together with him only in his boxers, it shouldn't be too weird for him to walk out there in only that.

Opening the door, he headed down the short hallway, his nose picking up the scent of bacon as he neared the bathroom. Oh, a woman after his heart, for sure. Making him breakfast.

He peeked inside the bathroom, his clothes nowhere in sight. Well, shit. He swore he left them in here.

Having no choice, he walked into the living room, finding the room empty. He could hear low music playing in the kitchen—of course, a peppy Christmas tune—and a sweet voice singing along with it.

He had decided he wanted all in with her. That meant he wanted her for the rest of his life. She'd have to get used to him walking around the place with only boxers on. Puffing up his chest, flexing a bit, because hey, he could make himself look good, he ventured into the kitchen.

"Good morning."

A tiny shriek sounded across the way, as Chasity jumped in front of the stove, the spatula popping up out of the pan and a few eggs flying to the floor.

He grinned. "Sorry. I didn't mean to startle you."

She placed a hand to her chest, small laughter escaping. "Totally didn't startle me."

A brow rose. "No? Not even a tiny bit." He glanced down at the floor, his grin widening. "So, your eggs like to hop out of the pan like that all the time?"

"It's just the way I make eggs."

This woman couldn't get any more adorable if she tried. Her hair was looped up behind her head in a messy bun. She wore a pair of black drawstring pants with her night-gown still on, but a light tan sweater dressed over it. Her cheeks were starting to blush a rosy red. He sort of loved it when she blushed by something he did or said. It made him want to elicit more of that out of her.

He edged closer to her, his smile growing as he did. Her own sweet smile started to emerge as the pinkish hue laced across her cheeks spread down her neck.

"I seem to have lost my clothes." He chuckled along with her as he planted his hands on her waist.

"That is a tragedy," she said, biting the bottom of her lip as her eyes trailed downward.

He kissed her, trying to make up for failing to do so last night. She didn't resist, arching her body into his.

Every delicious part fit perfectly in sync with his.

Damn. He wanted more. More of her. More of every-thing he could possibly get.

"Your clothes are in the dryer. I thought you might like to wear something clean this morning."

He pressed another kiss to her lips, then her cheek, making a slow path across her jaw. "Thank you. I appreciate that." His kisses kept on their trail, making their way to her neck. "You must've gotten up early."

A breathy moan slipped out. "I couldn't sleep."

His mouth landed near her ear and took a nibble, eliciting another delightful, breathy moan. Oh, she wanted more just as much as he did. Reaching behind her, he flipped the stove burner off, then extracted the spatula from her hand and laid it on the counter. All the while nibbling and tasting her skin. Learning the spots that made sweet, delicious noises escape.

"Next time you can't sleep, you wake me up."

Then he lifted his head and met her gaze.

"You looked so peaceful sleeping. I felt bad doing that."

Or she was afraid to, still unsure of how she felt about him. Not that he was going to suggest that or even ask for the real reason.

"Breakfast smells delicious."

"I hope you like bacon."

He bent his head and kissed her neck, trailing his tongue upward until he could lightly bite her ear. "I love bacon."

She shivered in his arms, another low moan echoing between them.

"I would love to devour..." He pressed kisses along her collarbone, moving her shirt and sweater as he did, "...you from head to toe. Then have some bacon."

She giggled and didn't resist when he slid her sweater off her shoulders and it plopped to the floor.

"Here, in the kitchen?" she asked, the hesitation clear in her tone, yet a bit of awe.

"I know we've both changed some in the last fifteen years, but one thing I remember is being very adventurous in finding places to have sex."

Oh, were they adventurous. To keep things a secret—something he had stupidly asked her to do—they had to get creative when they wanted to get it on.

In the back of his truck. In the cab of his truck. In her car in the back seat—super awkward. Down by the lake—in a secluded part in case others arrived. At the quarries, hidden between some rocks—not the most comfortable of places. Oddly enough, never in a bed.

He should rectify that. A nice, soft comfortable bed would be perfect.

He swooped her into his arms, garnering another surprise squeak to leave her mouth.

"What are you doing?" she said a bit breathless.

"Being super adventurous."

She bit her bottom lip again, then giggled. "Should I be worried we're about to have sex outside in the snow or something?"

He chuckled, not minding the idea at all. Maybe at Dragon Hill where their first beautiful kiss started them on this path. Fifteen years couldn't stop the amount of lust and desire running through his veins for her. He just had liked to pretend it could stop.

He walked down her hallway and set her gently on the bed. "I thought a bed might be fun for once."

She looked around her room, then nodded as a sweet smile lit up her face. "Wow, this is adventurous for us. A first."

She scooted backward on the bed until she hit the headboard while he took off his boxers. Not much for him to derobe. Then he climbed onto the bed and crawled toward her like a predator seeking his prey.

Her smile widened as her teeth dug into her bottom lip. Oh, she was waiting for him to devour her and lap her up like the delicious treat she was.

He helped her remove her nightgown and threw it behind him. Then he playfully grabbed her legs and scooted her until she was lying on her back. It elicited a delighted squeal from her that turned into laughter. Oh, he had missed her laugh. Her gorgeous smile. Her way of making his life brighter and merrier.

Her loose drawstring pants disappeared, and her black panties almost got ripped in half, he was so excited to get her deliriously naked.

Shifting his body down on hers, he kissed her lips.

"I missed this."

Then he swept his hand across her cheek.

"I missed you."

She said nothing at first. He didn't need her to say anything. He only needed her to know how much he missed her. Soon, he'd show her how sorry he was for screwing everything up between them. So many years lost because he couldn't man up and be his own person.

He started peppering small kisses across her neck as one hand found its way to her breast, the other gliding down to her hip.

"Wait...Stu."

Chasity's words came out in a pained, breathless tone.

He lifted his head, confused. The way she told him to wait sounded like she wanted to stop. And he would. He'd never force himself on her, no matter how much want and desire coursed through his body at the moment. But the way her eyes begged him to continue didn't jibe with her words.

"Yes?"

She inhaled deeply, then let it out slowly as a silly grin appeared. "Do you have any condoms? I don't. Not something I add to the grocery list very often."

A low chuckle pooled around them as he kissed her and then rolled off the bed. "Where'd you put my wallet before you washed my jeans?"

"It's sitting on the dining room table."

He winked and raced out of the bedroom to grab his wallet where he kept a spare condom. His heart raced, more so from anticipation, although it had started to race because he thought she was calling the whole thing off.

Merry Christmas to him. Because this was about to happen. He didn't need anything else this year.

He walked back into the room, tearing open the package and rolled on the condom as she watched him with eager eyes.

"Ready?"

He had to double-check. Because if she wasn't—or even hesitated—he'd wait. He didn't want to rush her. The last thing he wanted was to lose her again—for good.

"So ready," she said in a whispered breath.

Then he joined her on the bed, rubbing his hand up and down his cock a few times, loving the way her eyes followed the movement. He pressed close to her, kissing her softly, then started to work his magic with his fingers, getting her wet and ready. Their kiss turned hot and brighter as she rocked her hips to his delicate fingers. He rubbed and teased her until she bit his bottom lip, moaning loud.

His hand wove up, pausing to circle her nipple, then squeezed lightly.

"That was fast," he said with a chuckle as he trailed kisses down her chin.

"It's been a long time." Her eyes were closed as her cheeks bloomed a beautiful light shade of red.

He knew she hadn't been waiting for him to get his head out of his ass so they could try a real relationship. But he liked to hear she hadn't had sex in a long time. That meant there hadn't been many other guys after him. Actually, not something he wanted to think about—ever.

She was his.

Today. Tomorrow. Forever.

And he needed her more than anything now.

He positioned himself and took his time entering her, resting for a moment when he was fully inside. "It's been a long time for me, too. Just like I remembered; you feel so perfect."

Her eyes gradually opened, pure bliss shimmering in her oceanic depths. "What are you waiting for?"

"Savoring the moment."

Oh, he wanted to savor every delicious moment with her.

He started to thrust softly, taking his time to pull out and push back in as if he had all the time in the world. Her low moans, the way she grabbed his ass, pushing him to go faster didn't deter him. Like old times. They always moved fast and hurriedly just in case anyone spotted them. They hadn't wanted to get caught. Or he hadn't, anyway.

But he didn't care anymore. The entire town knew something was up with them now. They'd been spotted together at Dragon Hill. They had lunch at the diner. His truck was parked outside her apartment building. People knew.

And he didn't care.

So, he wanted to take his time and love her body like she was the most precious treasure in the world.

He rained light kisses across her jaw and down her neck

as he pumped in and out. She didn't stop grabbing his ass, but it felt like her urgency died down and she was more like holding on for dear life.

That's how he felt. He wanted to hold her until the end of time and never let go even after that.

Hold her for eternity and beyond.

"Stu..."

Her breathy moan urged him to pump harder, but still with aching patience.

"God, I missed you."

A light kiss to her neck.

"So damn much."

Another kiss to her jaw.

"I don't know how I lived without you."

A tender kiss to her cheek.

"I'm all in, Chasity. For the long haul. In case that wasn't clear."

Then a bruising kiss to her lips that swallowed her blissful moan.

He thrust in and out, hard, yet slow until he felt the rush of an avalanche hit him—quick and strong.

He tensed. Her nails scratched down his back telling him she got hit by the snow as much as he did. His low growls mingled with her sweet, delicate moans as he let the euphoric feeling sizzle throughout his veins.

Their kiss turned tender and light until he finally pulled his head back.

"I like it in a bed."

She giggled and swatted his ass. "It was very adventur-ous, indeed."

"Do you want to come with me to check on the dog?"

She rubbed his butt cheek where she had slapped it and

nodded. "I'd like that. Do you want to be even more adventurous and take a shower together?"

"You speak to my heart with your dangerous living. Yes. Let's do it."

After he finished at the vet, his next stop would be the drug store for more condoms. Because once with Chasity would not be enough.

"BENTLEY, you're forgetting your hat. It's cold out." Emma held out the brown knit hat as she held Tuck, their 7-month-old boy on her right side.

He paused at the door, a huge bout of love filling up his insides at the precious picture in front of him. He felt so blessed—truly, undeniably blessed. He had found a beautiful, courageous, smart woman to share his life with. They now had an amazing little boy who loved to find trouble. Taking after his mother already. His sweet, feisty Emma loved to give him trouble all the time.

Like now. Making sure he had his hat when he had no intention of chilling outside in the brutal cold. His head and ears would be fine from going to the house to his truck. Then to the truck to inside the clinic.

But since becoming a mom not so long ago, she had turned into a worrywart. Not just for Tuck, but him as well. He never liked to see her frown, so he usually caved into whatever she needed him to do.

"What would I do without you?" Bentley asked as he walked back over to her and grabbed the hat, plopping it on his head so she couldn't argue he didn't wear it.

"Forget your truck keys as well," she said with a silly smile, his truck keys now dangling from her free hand.

Well, shit. Not only had he been about to walk outside without a hat—totally could've lived without—he had been about to leave without his truck keys. Certainly wouldn't get anywhere without those...unless he chose to walk. No, thanks. Too long of a walk to the clinic.

Seriously, he would lose his head more often if he didn't have Emma to back him up on everything in life.

He took the keys, his lips dipping into a frown.

He'd had a terrible night's sleep, and not because Tuck was teething and having trouble sleeping at night. No, he never minded sitting up with his son, rocking him back to sleep in the chair in the corner of the room. Soft, soothing static sound in the background. Low light, just enough to see. Rubbing his back until the crying stopped and he was back in a semi-peaceful sleep. Sometimes Tuck would last the rest of the night. Sometimes, like last night, he woke up several times needing lots of soothing.

He didn't mind any of that. He and Emma took turns as well. But he hadn't gotten much sleep last night because his mind had been worried about the poor dog he hit. He still couldn't believe he hit the little guy. It broke his heart he even injured him a little bit. Sure, the roads were bad, slightly icy. Yeah, it was dark out and the lighting wasn't great. Okay, he hit the brakes and tried to avoid the dog once he caught sight of him. But that didn't make it okay.

Emma drew him closer, hugging him with a tenderness that always eased some of the pain he was feeling at the time. It wasn't always easy being a firefighter, and sometimes he came home after a bad day, wanting to be alone. She never let him wallow in his pain by himself. She didn't always speak, but her simple touch could help erase part of the ache that always centered in his chest from the horror of the day.

"It wasn't your fault. Jax would've called if the dog turned for the worse, but he didn't. He said the dog didn't suffer many injuries and he's resting." Then she lifted her head and kissed him. "So, that means drive safely and don't rush trying to get there."

"Never." Because he wasn't about to hit another dog or get himself hurt and lose the two most important people in his world.

He pressed a kiss against Tuck's forehead, which evoked a giggle from his son and some slobber down his chin as he removed his hand from his mouth. Then Tuck reached up and touched his cheek, something he'd probably seen Emma do often. A wet, gooey hand slid around, making him giggle this time. Saliva in the morning, on his cheek. Oh, the joys of fatherhood.

He kissed Emma hard, telling her thank you in the most delicious way for keeping his head on straight. Planted another kiss to Tuck's head, then walked to the door.

"I won't be long."

He walked outside, grateful Emma reminded him to take a hat. The wind pelted his cheeks with a slight bite. Jumping into his truck, he blasted the heat and headed toward the clinic. Although it was lightly snowing out—still from last night—the roads weren't too bad. The crew was doing well keeping up with plowing and salting the roads.

Not icy like last night.

The poor dog. He could only hope it was doing well and on the road to recovery.

He made it a short time later, not going over the speed limit once. Emma would be so proud of him.

He wasn't surprised when Stu's truck pulled in right after and parked next to him. Stu had said he'd be here in the morning and he never broke his word. What surprised him was Chasity jumping out of the passenger seat. He had heard a rumor they might have a thing going on, but that was the thing. When he heard rumors, he never believed them until he saw it for his own eyes.

"Morning, Stu," he said as he met them by the door. "Hi, Chasity."

They both exchanged greetings with him.

"How are you doing? You know it's not your fault, right?" Chasity said in the same kind of tone Emma used with him.

He kept hearing the words, but it was hard to accept. His truck hit the dog. His foot didn't hit the brake fast enough. His hands could've swerved the wrong way.

Before he could respond, not even having a good response—because it *was* his fault—Jax unlocked and opened the door.

"Come on in." He looked tired. Dark, round circles shaded his eyes, his hair sticking up on its ends as if he had routinely combed a hand through his hair.

That was Bentley's fault, too. If he wouldn't have hit the dog, he wouldn't have had to bring the dog here and Jax would've gotten a full night's sleep—not whatever amount he had managed to get. He knew Jax had a cot in the back-room where he held the injured pets recouping from surgery and whatnot. Whenever an animal was here overnight, someone from the clinic always stayed with them. He figured Jax had taken that task last night.

"So, what's the prognosis, Jax?" Bentley asked, afraid to even hear the answer despite what his text indicated a few hours ago.

"He's doing well. Sore leg, but not broken. A slight cut as well. It didn't require stitches, but I cleaned it and wrapped it up. He needs to take it easy for the next few days. I can keep him myself for the next few days, but then..." Jax waved his hand for all of them to follow him toward the back area.

"And then?" Bentley asked, the first in line behind him.

Jax opened the door and led them to a large cage where the dog lay asleep with his leg wrapped with white gauze. The dog looked peaceful. Although Bentley wondered about his temperament awake.

"Jax, and then?" Bentley demanded again. It came out more forcefully than he intended but he didn't like how Jax stopped talking.

Jax sighed. "And then I need to find him a home. He has no chip, so I can only assume no owner. I will check the local shelters later today when they open to double-check, but as of right now, he's a stray. I can't keep him. The best I can do is find him a home. You know that's not always easy, especially with strays like this."

Bentley hated the sound of this, especially the way Jax sounded so despondent. "And if you can't find him a home?"

"I'll find him one."

That sounded much better coming from Jax. More confident and sure of himself.

Bentley bent low, eyeing the dog, wishing he could take him. Emma was allergic, though.

"I'll take him."

Bentley stood up and turned toward Stu. "Seriously?"

Stu nodded. "I like dogs. And he deserves a good home. I'd like to think I can provide that."

Jax stepped forward and shook Stu's hand with the brightest smile. "You have just made my life so much easier. Thank you, Stu. I know he'll have a great home with you. He's a mix. Maybe poodle with a cocker spaniel, but both are great breeds, so he should be a good dog for you. Not too temperamental at all."

Stu knelt down to the cage with an energetic smile. "I never had a dog before. Not even as a child. I wouldn't even mind if he had an attitude problem. We all have one at some point, don't we?"

Bentley laughed first—figuring that was true—Jax and Chasity joined in.

"You should name him? Unless you did already," Chasity said, looking at Jax.

Jax shook his head, then nodded at Bentley, as if he should.

But it didn't feel right. If Stu had never had a dog before, he should be able to experience it all, and that included naming him.

"You pick, Stu."

Stu stood and looked at the dog, then at everyone else. "He has some very curly hair. He'll need a haircut for sure with how ratty and knotty it looks. I imagine the bath you gave him, Jax, was not easy." Jax chuckled with him, nodding in agreement. "Curley is a good name."

Bentley agreed.

A fine name, indeed.

11

———————

CHASITY MELTED into his embrace and let the kiss consume her. Just like she let him consume her body this morning.

Oh, she had missed that. Not that she hadn't had sex in the last fifteen years. She had. She dated a few guys here and there, but none had ever captured her heart like Stu.

He had taken her heart and never given it back. Which was why she worried he could break it all over again.

Although, she was trying not to worry about that and put trust in that he wouldn't walk away this time. He said he wouldn't.

He pulled away. She cupped his jaw, smoothing a hand across his scruffy cheek. He looked tired, yet happy.

He was now the proud owner of a dog. Something he never had. She wasn't sure why that surprised her when he said it, but it had. Her family had two dogs growing up. One beautiful German Shepard that had been her dad's before he met her mom, and died when she was five. After that, her dad said they could get another one—this time a pretty golden retriever, Buttercup. When her parents divorced, her dad took Buttercup with him. That had been hard to deal with as much as the divorce had. She lost two things at the time. The sense of family and her beloved pet.

"Thanks for going shopping with me," Stu said with a goofy grin.

"Anytime." Then she snatched another kiss because she couldn't help herself.

They had stopped at the local pet store and bought the place up. Stu had gone a little crazy. Pet bed, two of them. One for the bedroom and one for the living room. He said he wanted Curley to have comfort wherever they chilled out together. Dog bowls. Dog mat for the dog bowls. Toys galore. He hadn't been sure what Curley would like, so he bought a huge variety of squeaky toys, balls, and ropes. When they ventured into the treat aisle, he had gone nuts. She had to remind him that dogs needed nutrition, too—not just treats. He bought several bones and bags of snacks, plus two big bags of dog food. As soon as he brought Curley home, this dog was set to have the best home ever.

"I know it's a lot to ask, but..." He grinned sheepishly, his eyes turning downward for a second before meeting hers. "...can I come over again tonight after the bar closes?"

"Of course. I should go. I'm meeting my sister and grandpa for lunch."

She enjoyed visiting with her grandpa, but she wasn't sure how seeing her sister would go. Not after the argument they had yesterday over the phone about the man sitting next to her.

"Have a good day at work. I'll miss you." A delicious grin sparked across his face, telling her exactly what he would miss throughout the day.

He had said that a lot this morning. She loved hearing it every time it popped out of his mouth.

She displayed her own devious grin, then opened his truck door and hopped out. "Have a good day as well."

Then she shut the door and headed inside her apartment. She putzed around, cleaning up. Not that much needed to be cleaned, but she needed to keep herself occupied before she left and saw her sister.

She wasn't sure what she'd say either. She wasn't prepared to throw Stu out of her life because Hope didn't think it was a good idea. Okay, so she worked for his dad and he wasn't the best boss. That didn't mean she couldn't date his son. That didn't mean he was a bad guy, too.

Time flew by, and she was leaving her apartment to head to the retirement home.

She had hoped to see her grandpa first, maybe get some great wisdom out of him on how to proceed with Hope, except fate had other plans.

Hope was walking toward the entrance at the same time as her. They met by the doors and walked inside together. It was too cold out to be arguing in the low temperatures.

They bypassed Debrah because they didn't want to argue in front of her either. They both wanted to clear the air because they walked in silence toward their grandpa's apartment rather than the commons area where they knew he'd be waiting.

Chasity walked in first, followed by Hope who huffed, yet didn't say anything.

She turned around and crossed her arms, deciding she'd let Hope say the first thing. She wasn't the one in a tizzy anyway. It was Hope who had the problem.

"You're glowing. Which means you had sex. How could you?" Hope demanded as she mirrored her stance and crossed her arms.

Her eyes turned up as a blissful smile touched her lips. "Best morning sex ever. Can't wait to have more later."

"He's going to hurt you again."

"Is this how it's going to be all the time?" Chasity shook her head, hating they were fighting. "He's not his father."

"He hurt you once. He'll do it again."

They could go round and round in circles with this. That's what happened when an issue popped up between them. No one was ever a clear winner until one of them—usually her because Hope could be so pigheaded about things—caved and apologized.

But she wasn't caving this time. That meant she'd have to let Stu go and she wasn't willing to throw this second chance away. Just because her sister worked for his father and thought he was the world's worst boss.

"Are you upset because you think Stu is going to break my heart," she inhaled deeply, "or are you upset because I didn't tell you we were a thing years ago?"

Hope frowned and dropped her arms to her sides. "We never keep secrets from each other."

"Ha! I had to find out two months after you got your first tattoo. Damn it. I would've gotten one with you, and now I'll never get one."

Hope rolled her eyes. "First of all, you can come with me the next time I get a tattoo. It wasn't that bad. It's doable pain. Second of all, I told you two months later. Not *fifteen* years later. Big difference."

"So, there's the heart of the problem." She frowned, too. "I'm sorry, Hope. I didn't keep it from you to hurt you. It's...I thought he was the one that got away. It hurt to even think about him."

"And now you don't think he got away? You think you

reeled him in as a keeper this time?" Hope sounded skeptical.

Chasity could understand why. The horror stories she told all the time about Stu's dad were nuts. She couldn't believe the other townsfolk loved him as they did. They thought he was the world's best mayor. Yet, behind closed doors, behind the scenes, he was a grade-A jackass, especially to Hope. Chasity didn't understand why she kept working for him when he never had a nice thing to say to her. Made her work long hours. Kept her in the office on the weekends when everyone else had off.

Yet, Hope never voiced her displeasure or hatred for the man to anyone but her. As far as anyone else knew, she was happy at her job.

"I don't know, but I hope so. He makes me happy. He's nothing like his father."

"You don't know that."

Chasity slammed her hands to her hips. "In all your interactions with Stu, has he ever reminded you or displayed the same kind of behavior as his father?"

Hope huffed again. "No."

"Have you ever heard anything horrible about Stu? You know how gossip talks around here."

Another huff. "No."

"Well, then. Give him a chance. His last chance."

Something she told herself as well. Fool her once, shame on him. Fool her twice, well, shame on her. Fool her a third time, she was just plain dumb to give him a third time. If Stu broke her heart again, she wouldn't give him the time of day.

"Fine. But I'm not happy about it."

"I never said you had to be."

Then she held out her hands and Hope crossed the

distance and hugged her. Chasity apologized first, but Hope could take the first steps to true peace between them.

"Is anything else bugging you? I never imagined you'd get this upset about me dating Stu."

Hope averted eye contact as she took a step back. "No, I'm good. I don't want to see you get hurt."

Liar, liar, pants on fire. She almost said the old-age saying out loud, something they loved to say to each other growing up. But she held the words back because before Hope had looked away, she had seen a flash of pain. Of deep despair that she didn't understand. But she knew it had nothing to do with the issue with Stu.

"Ready to school Grandpa in a game of cards?"

"We never win against Grandpa. We only ever win if we're on his team," Hope said, the playfulness back in her voice. Then she put an arm around her shoulder. "Sorry for getting on your case. It's been a stressful few weeks. I took a lot of it out on you. Although, I do worry he will hurt you again."

"Hey, that's what sisters are for. I know you'll always have my back."

"Girl, that man won't know what hit him if he hurts you."

She half-groaned and giggled all in one with that loose statement. "Stop. Don't even say things like that. You're lucky Dale never found out you keyed his car."

"Peckerhead should've never cheated on me. I have other things up my sleeve I can dish out. So, Stu better be on his best behavior."

Oh, she loved her sister. But she had a wild side that scared her sometimes.

Poor Stu had no idea what he was getting himself into

dating her. But, Hope was right. She was afraid he'd break her heart again, too.

She'd keep this little tidbit to herself. Stu could find out on his own what might happen if he bailed once again.

BLOWING OUT A BREATH, he exited his vehicle. Although he forgot his hat, he took his time walking from his truck to his parents' front door. It was cold as shit out, the light wind hitting the top of his stitches gave him a sharp pain, but he didn't care. He definitely hadn't forgotten it on purpose because he didn't care if his hair got messed up from a hat that was supposed to keep his head warm. And his father always wanted him—and anyone else in his circle—to look presentable and put together. Mussy hair from a hat that most people wore during the winter was unacceptable to him.

Oh, how he wished Chasity were by his side. It would make this more bearable. But she'd also get an eyeful of his father. Of course, his father wouldn't be overtly rude, just his usual self. Expecting everyone to bend over backward to do his bidding and worship him as if he were a king.

Geez.

He was the mayor. But he was not royalty.

The day had started out so promising, too. Making love to Chasity with an added bonus of fun in the shower. Visiting the clinic to learn the dog—Curley, his dog—wasn't as badly injured as he and Bentley had assumed. Adopting said dog and providing him with the best home he could.

And now this.

Lunch with his parents.

There was no way he could say no to his mother. Especially when she used the most pitiful voice in her arsenal that would have him feeling bad for saying no.

When he finally reached the door, he exhaled another slow breath, then knocked. His mother always chided him for not simply entering, considering it was the home he grew up in. She said it still made it his home, but he felt awkward doing that. His father usually had a disdainful look on his face like he didn't agree. Maybe he should walk in, just to piss him off.

But he didn't always want to be fighting back and forth with his father.

Just once in his life, he wanted his father to see him. *Really* see him for the man he was. A bar owner. A business owner. A respected person of the community. But all his father ever saw was a disappointment that he wouldn't follow in his footsteps with politics. No. Thanks.

The door opened with what felt like an eternity but only ten seconds or so passed. His mother smiled brightly and pulled him inside, hugging him as if she hadn't seen him a few days ago.

"You look pale. Have you been taking it easy?"

Thirty-five years old and his mother still liked to treat him like he was five. He didn't mind. As her only son, he usually let her coddle him and do her thing because it made her happy, and he hated when his mother looked unhappy. Something he had been the cause of the last few holidays.

"I'm fine, Mom. I promise. I'm taking it easy. My head doesn't even hurt anymore. What's for lunch?"

She brushed a hand along the edge of his hairline, in that motherly way, yet he saw a bit of trepidation. Then she spoke.

"Your favorite. Sloppy joes with a side of chips."

Oh. Shit.

He should've declined lunch. His mother would never make his favorite unless his father wanted something from him. She hated sloppy joes. She only ever made it for him growing up because he loved it, and she spoiled him. He never minded being spoiled.

"Don't give me that look, mister," his mother said in a soft, berating tone.

Hiding his disgust at his father's antics didn't work. Not that he had tried too hard to hide his reaction.

"What does he want? At least give me a heads-up."

She puckered her lips as if debating whether she should or not. Then she patted his cheek. "I wish my two favorite men could get along. I do. That's what I would like for Christmas this year. For you to get along with your father."

He sighed, hating to disappoint her. Because as long as his father kept getting on his ass about things he didn't care about, they weren't going to get along.

"If he stopped to see me for who I am and not what he wants me to be, we could get along."

"He loves you, Stu. So much."

He barely repressed the urge to roll his eyes. But he'd never hurt his mother in that kind of way.

"Come on. Let's eat."

Then his mother walked away without giving him an inkling about what his father wanted. Just. Great. He was walking into the battle zone with no bullets or armor. Not fair. But life generally wasn't when it came to his father.

He followed his mother into the dining room where the table was already set. Napkin, forks, spoons, plates, and bowls, all in its place as if they were having some sort of formal dining. No half-assing anything in this household. His mother even used the good china.

Shit.

That did not bode well at all. His father wanted some-thing important from him.

"I'll go grab the food. Sit."

Not wanting to make his mother even more unhappy because he had yet to smile since he walked inside, he sat in his usual spot. To the left of his father's place, and across from his mother. His father always sat at the head of the table. Always trying to display his authority.

She left the room.

His father took that opportunity to enter and took a seat in his usual spot. No smile. No greeting. But he unleashed a heavy sigh as if Stu had done something wrong.

Maybe he had.

His mother hadn't walked out with a pleasant smile on her face, and she usually had one. She was a people person. Loved to converse with others. Make them laugh. Have small talk. She was the perfect wife to a man like his father —one who loved to be in the spotlight.

"You look terrible. That's what happens when you own a bar. Bar fights happen and you get hurt."

He leaned back, scoffing. "Oh, and you suddenly care that I get hurt?"

His father sighed again. "Must we always argue?"

"Gee, *Dad*, you sat down without a hello and immedi-ately started in on me why it's so terrible I own a bar. Some-thing I love. Tell me, who started that fight?"

"You know how I feel about the bar, Stewart. George never should've left that place to you."

Not that he hated his full name, but he liked going by Stu instead. Being his father, he never corrected him. He had given him the name, so he didn't want to be that disre-spectful. But considering everyone else called him Stu, one would think his father could try calling him that instead.

Plus, he always said it condescendingly, as if needling him with his own name.

"Is that why Mom made sloppy joes? So you could remind me for the billionth time why it's so terrible I own my own business? People like bars. People like alcohol. People like to socialize. I make good money. I own a nice establishment. People like my bar. And rarely do bar fights occur."

His father clasped his hands, sighing one more time, then averted his eyes.

That sighing. Why did he keep sighing? So unlike his father.

Also odd. His father always maintained eye contact. He was a stickler for that kind of thing. Said you could decipher a person with one glance. Their temperament. Their attitude. The way they'd react to something.

"I've been hearing you're seeing Chasity Bronson. Is this true?"

Oh, Stu did not like where this was headed.

Although Stu had pushed Chasity away all those years ago, afraid how his father would react—because his father was judgmental about every aspect of his life—he had never actually told Stu not to date her. He hadn't known. Nobody in town had known. In the end, he had pushed her away anyway. Because he didn't want to see her hurt and abused by this man. Because he didn't have the balls back then to stand up for what he wanted. To live his life the way he should.

"Yes."

His father turned his head, hitting his gaze direct on. "You need to stop seeing her."

"Excuse me?"

The man actually had the audacity to say that to him.

What could he possibly have against Chasity? Perhaps Stu hadn't been wrong to end things with her fifteen years ago. Because his father was currently proving his fears correct.

"I think I misheard you."

"You heard me fine. End—whatever is going on between you two—today."

He said it with such finality. Like Stu was a teenager about to be grounded if he didn't follow the rules. Well, he was no kid with no backbone any longer.

"No."

"Yes."

Stu chuckled, to hide the anger simmering to the surface. "No."

His father rubbed his chin, then grinned. "I'm running for governor. It's not going to look good my son owns a bar. It's not going to look good my son is dating a woman with a dysfunctional family."

Wow. This just blew the cake. Dysfunctional family? Her mom died five years ago from cancer, and her dad didn't even live in town anymore. He wasn't even sure what her dad was up to these days. They were divorced, long before her mother had even passed. But his father shouldn't think that was too dysfunctional. Lots of people got divorced these days. Another example of how extremely judgmental his father could be. Of people having to live up to his high standards. Too high.

Hell, her sister Hope worked for him. Shouldn't that mean something in Chasity's favor?

"Mom sure is taking a long time with those sloppy joes."

"Why must you always defy me?" His father said in a low tone as if he were trying to hide the rage wanting to unleash.

Stu stood up, shoving his chair back. "Why must you never see me as me? My own person. But no, it's always about you. How can I make you look better? Good luck running for governor. I won't be voting for you."

Then he walked out of the room and into the kitchen where his mother stood near the entryway eavesdropping.

"Really, Mom? That's what he wants. And you're on board with this?"

Her expression fell into remorse. "He said he wanted to speak to you about his campaign. I had no idea he'd ask you to stop seeing Chasity. I do not agree with that."

Stu stepped closer and kissed her cheek. "Thanks for lunch, Mom. I can't stay, though. Have a good day."

Then he left before he did something rash. Like, tell his father how much he hated him.

What a way to ruin his Christmas, but also his mom's.

12

"I LIKE THE ADDED CHRISTMAS CHEER," Bentley said as he sat on a stool, placing a small bag designed with reindeers all over it, bright red pompoms on each nose.

The bag was hideous. Stu couldn't help but laugh.

"You talking about my bar or that ridiculous bag you have there?" Stu said, laughing some more.

It felt good to laugh. He hadn't even smiled much since leaving his parents' house. Only a few bright spots had lightened his mood and that had been when he texted a few times with Chasity. But then she got busy with a call— something about a train stuck up a kid's nose—and his phone had been radio silence the last two hours. He sure hoped the child was okay and the train came out easy. Sounded like a good story later for her to regale. Children were curious creatures. But a train—up their nose? It sounded painful thinking about it.

Bentley wiggled the bag as he laughed along. "Emma bought it on a whim when she was shopping the other day with Lynn and Laura at this weird store in Mason—Wacky

Wowza's. I don't know what she was thinking, but she got such a kick out of it when she showed me."

Oh, yeah, Stu had been to that store a few times. They had everything. Clothes, food, antiques—a fun sex aisle. He had some good memories venturing in there as a teenager. He always went down the sex aisle to see how much he could embarrass his father, especially when he berated him for this or that minor thing. Getting a B in English. Yeah, that's how controlling and demanding his father could be. He expected perfect As in his son. No B to be had here.

"It's definitely...wacky," Stu said with a chuckle as he looked at the reindeers floating on the bag, the pompoms sticking out with flair. Not one reindeer had lost its nose.

"I didn't think you decorated for Christmas," Bentley said with a slight hesitation as if he wasn't sure he should broach the subject.

Stu glanced around at the few things he let Chasity hang up. He hadn't forgotten to turn on the lights—or off when he left—and they surprisingly lifted his spirits when he turned them on today. Because they made him think of Chasity, and she always made him happy when she penetrated his thoughts.

"Chasity convinced me to hang a few things up. I don't mind the decorations." He shrugged, not willing to explain any further.

"Yeah, I get it." Bentley nodded as if he did.

Stu wouldn't be surprised. He didn't talk about his father often. Not even in malice. The last thing he needed was his father breathing down his neck because he was badmouthing him around town. But on the rare occasion, he had confessed a time or two to Bentley, Aiden, and Elliot the discord between him and his father. Those three knew. They understood.

"Well, then," Bentley grinned wickedly, "you won't mind if I add a few more things."

Stu chuckled, but it was a mixture of laughter and a sigh because he wasn't sure if he should be worried or not.

"Oh, really?"

Bentley dug inside the outrageous bag and pulled out two mistletoes.

"I already have one of those near the front door."

A brow rose as Bentley set them on the bar. "I made these myself. I'm an expert mistletoe maker, so you're taking them. One can go by the pool table and another can go near the hallway leading to the bathrooms. Have a little fun with it, Stu. Don't be a Scrooge."

More laughter escaped as he picked one of the mistletoes up. It was shaped in a ball, holly mixed around with bright green leaves. A red ribbon rounded it out nicely, looped in a bow with a string to hang it up with.

"Since when did you get so crafty?"

Bentley grinned. "When Aiden needed to impress Theresa and beg for her forgiveness a few years back. Don't even ask how many we made then. Emma had craft night with Erin and her sister Aria the other night. I was there, James was there, and..." Bentley waved his hand at the mistletoe. "...this is what happened."

Now, that would've been a sight to see. James making mistletoe. He couldn't picture it. Not even for Erin.

"I feel like I should be nervous to see what else in that bag."

Bentley nodded with little naughty elves twinkling in his eyes. "My fiancée had way too much fun in Wacky Wowza's."

He proceeded to pull out a Santa sitting on a toilet. Then he pushed the toilet lever and a very merry song about Santa visiting the town and how you better watch out started playing as Santa reached to pull his pants up, then pull them back down. It had Stu cracking up with laughter, he had to wipe a few tears away.

Stu picked it up and pushed the lever again, laughing some more. "Okay, I like this decoration. This is a good one."

"Right," Bentley said with a bright smile. "I almost didn't want to part with that one, but Emma said I had to."

Next, came a string of Christmas lights, although the bulbs were shaped into cowboy boots. He wouldn't classify his bar as a country bar, but he did tend to play country more than anything else. And considering where Emma bought it, he wasn't surprised.

The last thing that came out was a Santa hat. Not very original, but he did raise a brow.

"You don't honestly expect me to wear that, do you?"

"Only on Christmas Eve, for sure. Since you're closed for Christmas Day." Bentley shrugged. "Or have whoever else is working that day to wear it."

Stu grabbed the hat and put it on. Why not? His father actually wouldn't approve of it, so it made him feel better to wear it. To spite him.

He still couldn't believe what his father wanted him to do. Expected him to do.

There was no way in hell he was giving up Chasity. Not after getting her back after all this time. Not after realizing he should've never given her up in the first place.

"Looks good on you." Bentley looked around, then nodded toward the large bay window. "How about I hang the lights there? I brought the supplies to make it happen."

"Oh, so I'd have no way to argue about it."

"Yep."

Stu nodded. "Hang away to your heart's content."

Bentley sauntered off across the room. Stu took the

Santa on the toilet and set it near a napkin dispenser in the middle of the bar. Why not give everyone the opportunity to play the ridiculous song. People would get a kick out of it and have a good chuckle. With how his day had been going, he needed all the merry cheer he could get.

When Bentley was done, he came back over and folded the bag, pushing it toward him. "You keep it. Pass it on to someone else."

What a grand idea. He could buy his father a gift this year. Oh, the reaction on his face if he tried to hand this to him. The stodgy old man. Always worried about appearances. Yet, pretending he loved the holiday when he was only using it to his advantage, getting people in his corner when they were full of spiked eggnog.

Then Bentley sighed. "Thanks for taking the dog. I like the name Curley. I visited him again earlier. He's up and walking." Bentley moved his head back and forth. "Slowly, but he's moving. He's very friendly."

"Of course. I like dogs. I don't know why I never got one before." Stu leaned forward, resting his forearms on the bar. "So, does Jax think I could pick him up tomorrow? I mean, he didn't call me. I didn't ask him yet. But you just saw him..." He let his voice trail off, knowing Bentley would understand what he was saying.

"Yeah, you could." Bentley winced. "Except Jax thinks it would be good if you're around the first few days. You know, so Curley can get used to his surroundings and such. Not be alone for half the day. You work."

Stu grinned. It didn't matter he had to work. He didn't like to think of Curley sitting in a clinic, sometimes in a cage, when he could be chilling in his new home.

"I'll figure something out. Thanks for the update."

Bentley stood up. "No, thank you. Seriously. It was

bugging me I couldn't take him myself. I know he'll have a good home with you. I better go. I told Emma I wouldn't be too long and I'd give Tuck his bath tonight."

"Thanks for the Christmas cheer." Then he reached over and flushed the toilet. Santa did his thing, pulling his pants up and down as the song sang out in the bar.

Bentley chuckled. "Anytime, my friend."

Stu wanted to take Santa home and show Chasity. He knew she'd get a good chuckle out of it herself.

His sweet, beautiful Chasity.

How was he going to tell her what his father asked of him? Because part of him felt like if he was going to try and make things work this second time around, he had to be completely honest with her. About everything. That included every nasty thing his father said or did.

He suddenly wasn't looking forward to tonight. He had no words.

CHASITY STROLLED into her apartment with a hand on her lower back. A slight twinge of pain lingered from when she stood up—the wrong way—at the little boy's house. Thankfully, with a pair of tweezers and a whole lot of prayers, they managed to get the tiny toy train he'd thought would be fun to stick up his nose out. It had been small, about an inch long and 1/2 inch thick. She had no idea how the little guy managed to get it up his nose, but nothing surprised her these days with the things people could manage. He hadn't needed to go to the hospital, so that was good.

It was a little past eleven. She'd have plenty of time to relax in the bath before Stu arrived. She didn't normally indulge in a bath, but her body was sore and it sounded soothing. Besides the toy train incident, they dealt with a crash victim—that *did* have to go to the hospital—and a few other minor calls that left her exhausted. Maybe she'd even read a book, get her mind off the day. The car accident hadn't been pretty.

While the roads were salted well, the past week it had been snowing off and on, making some parts difficult to manage. The poor mom driving her children of three hit a wrong patch in the road, sliding and jerking until she ran off the road and hit a tree. All the kids appeared to be fine, but she hit the tree on her side. They had to extract her out of the car carefully as her side of the vehicle crunched like an accordion.

There had been a lot of blood.

A lot of screaming.

It hurt her heart—pierced her with such brutal pain.

It wasn't always an easy job, but she enjoyed it. She liked helping people. Being there for them in a time of crisis.

She plugged in her Christmas tree in the corner of the room near the TV, smiling. Nothing like a bit of Christmas cheer to brighten her mood. Or at least mask it for a few minutes.

After grabbing a pair of pj's—a light tank top that said, "We wish you a merry sleep" and a matching set of shorts—she took a towel from the closet and started the bath. Sinking into the water, she sighed. A soothing, contented sigh. The water was hot, hitting all her sore muscles in the right way.

Then a defeated moan let loose.

She forgot to grab a book.

Oh, well. She'd relax and enjoy the way the water touched every muscle, the way the heat scorched her skin and brought her peace. Because when she took a bath, she made sure the water was as hot as it could be. The hotter, the better.

Closing her eyes, she let her mind relax. Or at least tried to. Instead of thinking of her crazy shift, she thought about Stu.

The way his eyes lit up when he saw her. His hazel eyes, reminding her of a good shot of whiskey—a bit of amber and gold, sparkling with intensity to take a sip. And always twinkling with a bit of mischief and desire. Such an odd mixture, but fit him well. He loved to tease her—in so many ways. Both fun, yet sexual.

Or the gorgeous way his lips curved into a devilish smile as if he had a secret he wouldn't be divulging until she begged on her knees to know it. Of course, the only begging to be had would be him to her. After the way he treated her all those years ago, she deserved him to grovel a tiny bit. But she had to admit, he was doing a good job of making amends and showing he cared.

It frightened her he could break her heart once more, but that was the thing about love, it was scary and terrifying. It also wasn't easy.

Just a quick look at her parents said it didn't always last.

That didn't mean it couldn't.

Although they had been apart for fifteen years—and had only two magical months together all those years ago— she knew Stu was the one for her. He made her pulse beat like a stampede of rhinos hell-bent on destruction. He made her skin tingle with anticipation. He made her heart soar as if she were the only person on earth that mattered.

She loved him.

It might not end well, but she was willing to take that leap of faith.

When she felt the water start to turn a bit cold, she knew

it was time to get out. She took her time rising, twisting her body this way and that, checking out all the kinks. No twinge of pain. A bath had been a great idea.

By the time she had put herself together and dressed in her pj's, the time said she only had about fifteen minutes or so until Stu should arrive. It had been a very long bath.

Curling onto the couch, she grabbed the remote, flipping through channels until she landed on a sappy Christmas movie that put an equally sappy smile on her face. She loved the feel-good Christmas movies this time of year. They could always brighten her mood as well.

A knock on the door jolted her out of her focus. The doctor of the small town was about to enact the sweetest "forgive me, come back home" gesture. It had taken the help of others in town to pull off the surprise to the sweet cookie maker he had fallen in love with. Of course, she was going to miss it as she had to answer the door. But that was okay.

Her own hero had arrived.

She pulled open the door, drinking in Stu's adorable, wicked grin that said she wouldn't be getting any sleep any time soon.

"I missed you. You have no idea." Then he stepped inside and wrapped an arm around her waist, kissing her, shoving the door closed behind him with his shoe. He dropped a duffle bag near their feet and wrapped his other arm around her waist, pulling her as close as he could.

She shivered. From a mixture of his tender kiss to the cold still emanating off him. His lips were chilly, like the first scoop from a tasty bowl of ice cream.

"Is that Christmas music I hear?" Stu said, in between pressing soft kisses against her lips. "I might be all Christmased out tonight."

She giggled, then turned her head to expose her neck

when his mouth started a new path, running light kisses across her chin and down her neck. "I was watching a movie and just missed the best part. Where they announce they love each other and have a merry Christmas."

He stiffened.

What did she say wrong?

Then he relaxed and met her gaze with a smile, although it didn't reach his eyes. No devilish merriment sparkled in his whiskey-colored eyes.

She didn't know what to say. Maybe she shouldn't say anything because it was late and she wasn't in the mood to argue—in case her inquiry to his odd behavior incited an argument.

"Why are you Christmased out?" she asked, adding a touch of laughter to lighten his spirits once again.

Stu rolled his eyes, but also added his own laughter. It sounded pure, thankfully.

"Word got around fast that you put up a few decorations in the bar. Bentley stopped by with a few things." His smile brightened, a true honest smile this time that reached his eyes and made her feel better. Awkward moment gone. "Then Aiden and Theresa popped in. Next came in Elliot, and a few other folks that couldn't help themselves. It's like Christmas puked in my bar."

She slapped his shoulder playfully, laughing. "It can't be that bad."

"Just wait and see. You can come see it in the morning."

She grabbed his hand and ventured into her living room where she gestured for him to take off his coat. "Or I can stop by after my shift. Are you hungry? I can make you a quick sandwich or something."

"Nah, I'm good." He hung his jacket in the closet in the hallway, then grinned. "I have the next few days off. It feels

weird, but Marcy—who was working with me tonight—
insisted I take off. Bentley told me Curley can come home
tomorrow but he should have someone with him for the
first few days. Get him used to his surroundings and whatnot. So, looks like I'm chilling at home for Christmas. Marcy
and Phil are going to hold down the fort for me. I feel bad,
but they didn't seem to mind. Actually, they wouldn't let me
argue about it."

She wrapped her arms around him, happiness filling
her up. "That's so wonderful to hear. That little guy is all set.
You bought the entire store up."

He shrugged, sheepishly looking away. "I couldn't help
myself. It's no big deal."

"He is going to be one spoiled dog." Then she swiped a
hand through his thick brown hair, relishing in the way he
closed his eyes as if he enjoyed it.

"I'm exhausted. It was a—" He paused, sighing. "It was a
long day. You ready to crash?"

"Of course."

He kissed her, then stepped out of her embrace. "I need
to use the bathroom."

"I'll keep your spot warm."

He walked out of the room. She kept her smile in place
until he disappeared and she heard the door shut.

Something was off with him. He was saying the right
things. Smiling as if all was right. Yet, something was both-
ering him.

Big question was, would he share with her?

She locked the door, shut off the lights and TV,
unplugged the Christmas tree, and slid under the covers,
snuggling into his side of the bed.

He joined her a few minutes later, hopping into bed and
pulling her closer without hesitation.

The lights were out. Only a sliver of light shone through her bedroom window above their heads from the streetlamp on the end of the street.

But she didn't need light to feel the tension radiating off him.

"What's the matter?" She brushed his scruffy cheek, worried once again. "Did I say something wrong?"

"You're perfect, Chasity. I knew that from the moment I met you."

"Stu—"

"Everything's fine. I promise. Let's get some sleep. Big day tomorrow."

Then he kissed her before she could argue. But again, she didn't want to argue with him. Something was wrong. She wasn't an idiot. Call it woman's intuition. A woman could always tell when something was off. But instead of forcing out the issue, she kissed him back, trying to release her tension so she'd be able to sleep. When he was ready, he'd tell her what was going on.

Hopefully.

13

STU WOKE up with a giddiness he hadn't felt in a while. He was a dog owner. How many times growing up had he begged and begged his parents—usually his mom because he thought she might be able to convince his father—and heard the answer no? Way too many times, he didn't even bother to count.

Today was the end of that. Odd, why he never thought about getting a dog before this. He was a grown adult. Had been for a long time now. He could've gotten a dog at any point, yet it took this incident for it to happen.

Well, whatever. He wasn't going to analyze his prior decisions. Things were changing now and that's all that mattered.

"I can feel you vibrating with excitement in my arms," Chasity said in a sleepy voice, pressing a light kiss to his chest.

"Today's the day." He didn't even try to keep the excitement out of his voice. He was damn excited.

Today was the day for a few things. He needed to have a talk with Chasity about his father and what he said to him.

But not yet.

He didn't want to ruin his morning. And that conversation could ruin the entire day.

He kissed her forehead, snuggling her closer. "You work today, huh?"

"Yeah." She started to trace a finger around his chest.

It didn't have a particular pattern. Just randomly brushing her finger here and there, tickling him in a few spots. Yet, her touch—even if it was a bit ticklish—always made him yearn for more.

"Well, let's not waste any part of this day."

His fingers glided down her backside in a slow caress until he stopped at the edge of her panties. She shivered in response, a low throaty moan echoing in the early morning air. His hand wove its way to her hot core already deliciously wet.

Turning slightly, his lips met hers as his fingers started to work their magic, eliciting tiny moan after moan from her sweet lips.

"My breath..." she whispered in between kisses.

"Yeah, my breath, too," he responded.

He didn't care they hadn't brushed their teeth yet. If he wanted to kiss her, he would. He'd missed having her in his arms and he wasn't going to regret any moment anymore. When it came to anything.

He pushed a good woman away.

He never bought a dog.

He never decorated his bar for Christmas.

All those things were changing, and he'd never hold back like that again.

A finger dove inside her, then another as he brought her to the brink of madness. Her body arched his way, a loud moan escaping as she clutched his back, scratching her fingers down brutally.

Oh, he loved it when she came. Such a beautiful, glorious moment every single time. The way she moaned. The way she tensed, her fingers digging into him, telling him how wonderful it felt.

He wanted this forever.

She relaxed, her eyes opening.

"Good morning to me." Then she giggled, stretching her body like a cat.

Oh, yes. Good morning to her.

Then he removed her tank top, shorts, and panties, as well as his clothes, and grabbed a condom from the nightstand.

A sly, wicked smirk touched her lips as she took the condom from him.

"My turn."

Then she proceeded to roll the condom on with slow precision, driving him out of his mind. Her soft touch drove him wild. He wanted to thrust into her and go mad. Mark her so thoroughly, no one would ever question or wonder that she was his.

His.

He needed her, more than he needed his next breath. Rolling over, she giggled as he hovered above her.

"Now, my turn," he whispered close to her lips, kissing her softly. Then he entered her, relishing for a moment in how perfect she fit with him.

Then he went completely wild.

Thrust in and out with abandon. No control. No holding back.

She wrapped her sweet arms around him and held on, matching his pace and coming with him for the intense ride.

Her fingers dug into his back, her heels pushing into his ass. Just the way he liked it. As if she had to cling to him or she'd lose him.

Nope.

Never.

She would never lose him again.

His head fell onto the pillow next to hers, his hot breath fanning her neck. He was moving so fast, he could do nothing but hold her tightly and let the wondrous feeling vibrate throughout his entire body.

He felt so free. Holding the woman he loved, showing her how much he loved her, and that he always would. He'd leave his mark so she'd never forget.

God, he loved her.

He was an idiot for not realizing it much, much sooner.

"So close, Stu," Chasity whispered, her fingers dragging down his back in sweet, sweet torture.

So was he, but if he could hold out for her to come a second time, he would. He felt beads of sweat forming on his forehead, one droplet sliding down. He was like a wild stallion running from capture, refusing to bow down.

Then she tensed, moaning fiercely.

He broke free with her, letting the sensation course through his skin, filling him up with intense bliss.

He lost his energy. Instead of crushing her with his weight, he twisted so he wasn't on top of her, although still close enough his heavy breathing pushed small tendrils of her hair framing her face.

"Wow," she said breathlessly with a slight chuckle mixed in.

"Yeah, wow."

It was way more than wow, but neither of them had the proper words to explain what happened there. No simple morning sex for them. Oh, no. Earth-shattering, mind-blowing, soul-crushing sex was more like it.

God, he seriously loved this woman.

He'd tell her tonight—along with how dirty his father could be.

"Oh, he's so adorable." Chasity knelt down and scratched Curley behind the ear. He seemed to love it, bending his head and moving closer.

He had a slight limp, but overall, he was walking well on all four legs. Jax had given him a haircut because his hair had been too tangled not to. He wasn't so curly anymore, but those beautiful curls would grow back, and then Stu could decide how much he'd want to trim off next time.

"Thanks so much, Jax. He looks good." Stu knelt beside her, petting Curley on the other side of his head.

Maybe he knew who his new owner was because he switched tactics and went right in between Stu's legs, putting his front paws on his knees, looking for more snuggles and scratches.

"He's a little underweight. Don't give him too much food at one time. Slowly increase his diet. Keep an eye on his leg. If the limp seems to worsen or he's struggling to walk, bring him back in right away."

Stu looked up and nodded at Jax. He'd have an eagle eye on this little guy. For the next few days, they would be attached to the hip. He'd even let him sleep in the bed. He could already imagine what his father would say about something like that.

"All right, well, we'll get out of your hair. Chasity has to get ready for work soon."

Stu was grateful she decided to come with him to pick up Curley. After the most amazing time in bed with her, they got up, had breakfast, and a delightful time in the shower together. Then she said she'd like to get Curley with him. They stopped at his house first where he grabbed a leash and Curley's new collar, and he also gave her a spare house key.

It shocked her.

It kind of shocked him as well, but as soon as the key hit her palm, he knew he made the right decision. The only decision. If he wanted to move forward into a relationship that turned into forever, this was a good step to start with. To show her how he really felt. He didn't give his house key to just anyone.

He picked up Curley, said goodbye to Jax and Clara, and followed Chasity out of the building, who held the door open for him and also opened his truck door.

"Hop in first and he can sit on your lap. Is that okay?"

Her ocean-blue eyes shimmered with tenderness. "Of course, silly. He's such a snuggle bug, the way he tried to climb onto your lap. I want to hold him."

Maybe he was being a little overprotective of the little guy, but he preferred to carry him and give him as much attention and affection as he could get.

She climbed in, grabbed a blanket from the back, and positioned it on her legs. Stu set Curley down carefully, who whimpered and nudged his hand as if saying, "Where are you going?" He patted his head and bent down to kiss the top of his furry head.

"I'm right here, big guy. We're going home and me and you can cuddle on the couch watching some action flicks. I promise. Trust me, you want snuggles from Chasity, too. She gives the best hugs."

He looked at her with a wicked smile, wanting a hug from her. She chuckled. He winked, eliciting more sweet laughter from her.

Then he kissed her on the lips, laughing. "Oops. Should I kiss you after kissing Curley?"

She joined in laughing. "Well, too late to ask, isn't it?" Then she wrapped a hand around his neck, pulling him closer for another kiss. "Let's get going, troublemaker."

He closed her door, more laughter springing free as he watched Curley pop his head up and his eyes follow him until he rounded the vehicle. Curley looked at him when he climbed in, and he swore a smile graced his furry face. The dog was just too cute.

The drive home was filled with more laughter as Chasity snuggled with Curley, petted him, and got a face full of doggy kisses. Stu had to keep his full attention on the road as it decided to start lightly snowing once again. Although, the roads weren't bad. He was starting to get sick of this snow every single day. Just get it over with. Dump them with a bunch of snow and stop. The sprinkles here and there was getting old.

Once home, he picked up Curley and let Chasity lead the way once again where she unlocked and opened his door. He decided to set Curley down in the living room where he immediately started to roam around, sniff, and explore. He found his doggy bed near the couch, sniffed it, then stepped on it, circled a few times, and sat down. He propped his furry chin on the edge of the bed, looking at Stu with happiness. Like he was saying, *Thanks, man, for giving me a home.*

Stu nodded. "You're welcome, Curley."

"Well, I better get going. My shift starts earlier today. It's going to be a long day." She bent down near Curley and scratched under his chin. "I'd rather be hanging with you two cute guys."

Then she stood up and walked into his open arms.

"Unless you're too tired, I'd love it if you came here after your shift." He sealed his request with a promising kiss. Of much, much more of that to come if she came over.

"Sounds good."

With one more intense kiss, she left.

He looked at Curley. "What do you want to do? Should we watch a movie? Let me know when you have to go to the bathroom." Stu pointed toward the dining room where a set of sliding doors made entrance to the deck and the backyard.

He had already shoveled off the three steps from the deck to the yard. If it seemed to be too much for Curley, he'd walk him down the steps. He even shoveled a small little area for him to do his business. Everything was ready to go for him. Curley just had to do his part and let him know he had to go. Here's to hoping he understood that. In a little bit, he'd take him outside to show him and to get him familiar with the area.

Stu decided to grab a drink, although not quite ready for lunch. He winked at Curley, told him he'd be right back, and headed for the kitchen. Grabbing a pop from the fridge, he jumped a little when he closed the door and found Curley standing right there.

"You okay? How was the walk? Not too bad?"

Curley moved closer, nudging his leg as if asking for a pet, which Stu obliged.

"New surroundings. I get it, buddy. We're in this together, though. A whole day of nothing." Stu laughed.

He wasn't used to sitting idly around. Usually, he was at the bar, most times than not, or he was helping out somewhere around town, or hanging with Elliot or a few other friends. He didn't generally chill out at home, even though he had a nice three-bedroom house on the outskirts of town. When he was home, he enjoyed being outside, doing projects around the yard, or wandering around the woods enjoying nature. He liked to keep busy. These next few days would be interesting for him—and Curley.

"Well, since you're in here, let me show you where your food is at."

Stu waved his hand, as if he understood him, and walked to the other side of the island facing toward the dining room. It had a nice little enclave on the bottom, which his food and water bowl fit perfectly.

"Hankering for a bite to eat, or thirsty, head over here."

Curley eyed it, then stepped closer and took a few little laps of water.

"All right, got that taken care of. Movie time?"

His little tail starting waging. Stu was going to take that as a yes.

"Let's try this whole relaxing thing other people do. Think we have what it takes?" Stu asked him with a chuckle as he sat down on the couch.

Curley hopped up next to him, sitting right by his thigh. His head dropped to the top of his thigh and his little doggy eyes looked up at him adoration.

"You're right. We got this. Let's see what we can find."

Then Stu leaned forward, grabbed the controller, and tried to empty his mind of everything. Even the conversation he'd have to have with Chasity tonight.

Talking about his dad, especially the terrible thing he said about her family, was not high on his list of things to do.

But sometimes you had to do things you didn't want to. And he swore he'd never lie to her again.

For the time being, things were good. He'd focus on that. Later, he'd think of the right words he'd say to her. Because nobody would want to hear how callously his father put her down.

14

———

"I'll be quick. You want one?" Doug asked. The door to the ambulance stood wide open as he waited for her answer.

While the temperatures were the same as the day before, it felt even more brutally cold to her. She'd rather be with Stu and Curley, cuddling under a blanket on the couch while they watched whatever happened to be on TV. Stu didn't seem like the Christmas movie kind of guy, even though she loved the cheesy holiday movies that played on repeat every year. Theresa wasn't even working, so the coffee would be good. She'd rather have Theresa's sludge than delicious tasting coffee.

"I'm good. Thanks, though."

Doug nodded and slammed the door, heading toward the diner. Their shift started about an hour ago, and they had already responded to one call of a possible heart attack. Of course, it hadn't been anything close to that. But the sweet older woman thought so as her heart had raced after a mouse ran across her path, hiding in one of her bottom kitchen cupboards. Doug, being her hero, checked the cupboard she swore it ran into, coming up empty of any vermin. He set some mousetraps in the back and around her kitchen. By the time he finished, the older woman's pulse had dropped back to normal and she felt much better. She declined a trip to the hospital.

Chasity swore if that was how her entire shift was going to go, it would be a very long day.

Glancing out the window, she saw her sister Hope get out of her car a few parking slots away from them. Hopping out of the ambulance, bristling at the brisk wind that slapped her face, she shouted, "Hope!"

Her sister turned around, smiling.

Whew. So they were still good. Although they had talked it out, she knew her sister still wasn't too happy she was dating Stu. If he broke her heart, then lesson learned. She'd never give her heart to him again.

They hugged. Not because they normally hugged, but sometimes they had a strange pull toward each other as if sensing the other needed one.

"Why are you working today? I thought you had it off?"

Hope rolled her eyes. "Because I work for a beast. He demanded I had to come in today to finish some paperwork that couldn't be put off until after the holidays."

Chasity didn't know how to respond to that. She knew Stu didn't get along well with his father, but did she have to talk bad about him? Hope never had anything nice to say about the mayor.

"Sorry to hear that."

"How is Beast, Jr.?"

This time Chasity rolled her eyes. "Seriously? He is not his father."

Hope pursed her lips, then formed them into a pouty expression. "I'm not in the best of moods." She shrugged. "Sorry."

Yeah, well, considering Hope had told her yesterday she had off until the twenty-sixth for Christmas, she understood why she was grumpy.

"Is this a bad time to ask if you mind if Stu joins us for Christmas dinner with Grandpa?"

Not that she had asked Stu yet, but she wanted to. She knew her grandfather wouldn't mind.

Hope laughed. "Umm...yeah. You're brave, girl."

Her laughter joined her sister's. She knew it was a dumb thing to ask when her sister wasn't in the best of moods, but she also knew she'd get a chuckle out of it.

Then Hope sighed. "I'm feeling pissy. His dad is such an ass, but I know Stu's not that bad. Of course, I don't mind." Hope reached out and touched her arm. "I hope you know what you're doing. I heard...rumors."

Chasity tensed. Her sister never fed into rumors around town. Neither did she. Half of them were debunked and stupid. The other half wasn't anyone's business. Like the fact she and Stu started dating. Why should the town care? Mind your own business was what she wanted to tell everyone.

"Like?"

Hope twisted her lips, then bit the bottom one. "His dad is going to run for governor. I overheard him say Stu was going to help with the campaign."

"I doubt that."

She seriously doubted that. Stu loved his bar. He loved this small town. She wasn't sure what one did to run for governor, but could they do it in a small town like Mulberry? Probably not.

If so, where? Would Stu move away? They just got back together.

Hope shrugged. "I'm telling you what I heard. I'm not saying it's true. But…" She winced. "Be careful."

Of her heart. Yeah, she got the message.

"He's really running for governor?"

Maybe Chasity misheard her sister. Because something that big, she figured Stu would've already known. It was his dad, after all. Why hadn't he told her?

Before Hope could reply, another nauseating voice popped in.

"Of course, he is. It's going to be so exciting."

Chasity looked behind her sister to see Marybeth standing there. She couldn't stand Marybeth and only tolerated her in small doses. The woman was a viper of the worst kind. Spoiled, self-centered, and lazy. She didn't do anything but live off her father's money and make waves around town. Like now.

"Good afternoon, Marybeth. Have a good day."

Chasity didn't think she'd take the brush off, but it was worth a try.

"The campaign is going to be amazing. Especially with myself by Stu's side." Marybeth smirked wide. "Have a good day."

She continued to saunter down the sidewalk, as well as one could saunter on a shoveled sidewalk, with a devious smirk riddled on her face.

Hope rolled her eyes again. "Ignore her. Anything that comes out of her mouth is a complete lie. Stu would never be caught dead with that woman."

Except if it made his father's campaign look good. Her father was part of the city council. He had ties to Washington DC. He had many allies. If Mayor Hafferty wanted him and his entire family to look good, Stu dating the daughter of an influential man in town would look good.

But Hope was right. She couldn't see Stu complying with that plan, especially not with Marybeth. She was always stirring the pot and causing problems wherever she went.

"But the campaign isn't a lie. Stu probably knows."

Hope's eyes cast downward. Which told Chasity enough. That her sister agreed but didn't want to hurt her feelings and say it out loud she agreed.

"Hey, you should get to work before the beast takes his claws out," Chasity said with a laugh. "Doug should be almost done anyway."

"I love you. I'm always here for you." Then Hope grabbed another hug, this time in comfort.

Geez. She sincerely hoped her sister didn't have to be there for her—with a bottle of tequila to mend her broken heart.

They broke apart and said goodbye. Hope headed down the sidewalk. She hopped back into the ambulance.

Amazing how one small interaction could have her going from anticipating seeing Stu to dreading seeing him.

Damn. This was going to be a long day.

SMALL CLICKS TRAILED behind him as he headed for the front door. He had heard a car door slam. Chasity was finally here. Stu didn't think Curley following him was a sign of how excited he was to see her like him. Because he had followed him everywhere in the house the entire day. He went to the bathroom. So did Curley. He went to the bedroom to change shirts after spilling chili on the front. So did Curley. He went to the kitchen to refill his glass. So did Curley. The sweet little guy wouldn't leave his side.

He opened the door just as she stepped on the porch.

She jerked in surprise, frowning. Then like a light switch, she smiled. But it didn't reach her eyes. Odd.

Maybe she had a bad day at work.

"Sorry, didn't mean to startle you," Stu said as she walked inside and he closed the door. "We missed you today."

She turned his way, a smile still displayed, but the magic in her eyes empty. He leaned closer and kissed her, trying not to let her odd behavior get him down.

"I missed you, too." But she said it as she bent down to pet Curley behind the ears. The way she didn't make eye contact with him made him think she had been talking to Curley only.

Perhaps he needed to move their talk up to now because he didn't like the nervous energy floating between them.

"Everything okay?"

She stood and nodded. "It was an exhausting day."

He had no doubt, she looked tired. Beautiful, even with light dark circles under her eyes, but tired. Could that be the only reason for her odd behavior?

"Do you want something to eat?"

"No. A shower would be nice."

His body reacted to that, his cock coming to attention. Yes, please. He'd like a shower, too.

Then he noticed she didn't have a bag with her. No spare clothes. Not that he wouldn't let her borrow some of his clothes.

"But we should talk first."

Damn.

So, he hadn't been imagining her weird behavior. Something was wrong.

"Yeah, we should." Now was as good as any time to tell her about his father.

He gestured for her to follow him once she took off her shoes and hung her coat up in the closet near the door. He grabbed two beers from the fridge and sat down by her on the couch, handing her one of the beers. Curley had followed him the entire time. He jumped up, circled once, then sat next to him, resting his chin on his thigh.

He knew Curley liked to snuggle, but maybe he also knew he needed his comfort as well.

This conversation could go two ways.

She understood and spent the night.

Or...

She ended things now and left.

Chasity took a long pull from the beer, sighing.

"Must've been a *really* exhausting day," he said lightly, then taking a small sip of his own.

Turning to him, she frowned, her hand tightening on the bottle. He could tell by the way her knuckles suddenly turned white.

"What are we doing here?"

"Talking..." That was a loaded question and he didn't know how to answer. He wanted to tread lightly here and not say the wrong thing.

"Us, Stu? What are we doing?"

Leaning forward, he set his beer on the coffee table and then grabbed her free hand. "Heading toward a future, I hope. I messed up fifteen years ago. I admit it. I'm sorry I ever pushed you out of my life and the things I said. I'm sorry I hurt you. But I want this to work between us."

"Then we need to be honest with each other."

His brows furrowed low. The way she had her head tilted a fraction, the way her eyes narrowed just a titch, said she thought he lied to her about something. That he was being dishonest in some way.

"I have been."

Besides what your father said to you. The bastard.

"Have you?"

Well, shit. Had his father done something? Said something? He figured if something like that would've happened, he would've gotten a phone call from one of his friends. They wouldn't leave him hanging on the lurch while rumors floated around, especially since they knew he was chilling at home with Curley.

"Yes."

She looked down at their joined hands, then back up to him. "Is your father running for governor?"

Wow. News traveled fast. But would his father say what he said directly to Chasity?

"He told me yesterday he was. What does that have to do with us?"

Shit. He was acting like an idiot. But what good would come from telling her what his father said about her and her family? It was an insult. The last thing he wanted to do was hurt her feelings. He'd never drop her from his life again, not for his father. One mistake doing that was enough.

Low laughter spilled from her sweet kissable lips as her eyes finally—finally—sparkled with a touch of happiness. "I don't know. I saw Marybeth today and she said things I let get to my head for a moment."

He rolled his eyes. He could only imagine. That woman was always trying to set her eyes on a new man, even if they weren't single.

"Look, never believe anything that woman says. I learned that a long time ago."

They laughed together. Because it was true.

Even though she seemed to be back on track with being happy with him, he felt a strange tension in the air.

He should tell her.

Nope, bad idea.

It would fester and grow if he didn't.

She doesn't need to know.

Back and forth his mind went with the decision of whether or not he should say anything.

She smiled, then glanced around his living room, her eyes landing on his semi-small tree—he had felt bad for the poor thing. Droopy limbs, smaller than the rest in the plot. He didn't think anyone would take it and he hadn't wanted to see it not see the inside of a house. Sitting outside in the brutal cold, dying by itself. He might've never decorated the bar for Christmas, but he put up a tree and a few decorations given to him over the years from family and friends, mostly from his mom. Since she visited him quite often, he never wanted to hurt her feelings that he didn't appreciate her gifts. But he wasn't dumb. He knew his mother did it for that reason alone.

"That's a sad looking tree." Her smile deepened. "Yet, you managed to make it beautiful. The white lights look great on it. I like the Rudolph with his blinking red nose ornament."

Elliot, Lynn, and Laura had given him that three years ago. For some reason, it had reminded Laura of him, and she had to buy it and give it to him. She was as giving as her mother, and he had adored the gift, even though he still couldn't figure out why she had thought of him in the first place.

"Thanks."

Chasity chuckled, scrunching her nose in delight at Curley, who picked up his head as if begging for a rub. He obliged him by letting go of her hand and letting her pet him.

"How did your day go? How is his leg?"

"Good. We had a great day doing absolutely nothing. It was very odd. I'm used to being busy. Usually with the bar. Although I checked in with Marcy a few times. The last time I called she told me she'd quit on the spot if I didn't stop calling."

Chasity laughed with him. "What an odd threat." Her eyes twinkled with merriment. "But it worked, didn't it?"

"She's working hard to get her degree, doing online classes and stuff. She needs the job."

Awkward silence suddenly filled up the room, and he wasn't even sure why.

"Chasity..." What was he doing? He shouldn't say anything.

"Yeah?"

He looked down at Curley, and honest to God it looked like he was smiling encouragingly as if saying, *Dude, just tell her. Get it over with.*

Then he looked up at her.

"Why did you say I told you years ago you weren't good enough for me?"

She eyed him warily, her brows puckered, her lips tight. Probably wondering why he asked that question. When she first said it a few days ago, he wanted answers then. Yet, they never had the conversation.

It was time.

It was time to lay it all out.

Time to put his heart on the line.

"Because that's what you said to me."

He shook his head. "I never said those words to you."

Sure, he had said they'd never work. Back then, with his

father in his face about everything—everything—they wouldn't have worked. The stress would've been too much for him to deal with. He had gotten much better at compartmentalizing that.

But he never said she wasn't good enough for him.

She looked away. "You said we'd never work as a couple. You said it was just some summer fun. You said we were on different paths that just didn't connect." Her eyes sought his out. "You didn't have to say the exact words. It was how you said it when you said that last one."

Yeah, he was an asshole back then. Instead of facing the issues head-on, he let his fear of his father rule his life. All the way up until his uncle died.

"I'm sorry. I was a coward back then. My father—" He shook his head again. How did he even start? Where to start?

"My father is a controlling bastard. All my life, he's wanted to mold me into a mini him. I refuse to follow that path. Back then," he shrugged, "I had no backbone. I didn't necessarily follow his path, but I also didn't do things that would set his sights on me."

"Dating me publicly would've been a bad thing?"

Well, if he hadn't wondered before, he knew now it would've been.

"I didn't want to tarnish your life with the toxicity from mine. He was always on my ass to quit working at the bar and do something meaningful with my life. To spite him, I ignored him most of the time and I let my uncle take most of the hits for me. It's not that it would've been a bad thing, it just...I didn't want to put you through that. That summer was the only summer I was ever truly happy. I can fake happiness when I need to. That summer, there was nothing fake of how much I enjoyed being with you."

Chasity reached out and touched his bristled cheek. "Is he that bad? I never hear these things about him."

"He's a monster behind closed doors. He'd never show the public the real side of him."

She leaned forward and brushed her lips against his. It was too short and he wanted to pull her back into his arms, but he couldn't. He'd gone this far; he might as well keep going.

"When my uncle died and left me the bar, it was a brutal nightmare. Not because one of the best men I have ever known was gone and never coming back, but because I was a business owner. A bar owner. My father hated it. He thought with my uncle gone, it'd be easier to wield me into his clutches. He was wrong. I put my every last working minute of the day into that bar just to stay clear of him. I love that bar."

"I know you do. I can tell. It's *the* bar in town."

Stu chuckled with her. "It's the only bar in town."

"Yes, but there's a few not far away, but yours is always busy." She smiled, then laid a comforting hand over his. "I never imagined he was that controlling. I'm sorry. My dad can be frustrating, but never that bad."

"I should've apologized to you years ago. I should've explained everything days ago. There's more."

"Okay." She slowly removed her hand as she took another large sip of her beer.

He ran a hand through his hair, dreading this part.

"I'm no coward anymore. I don't let my father control my actions. I used to and I regret it."

"Okay."

Shit. He shouldn't tell her.

But he didn't want any lies between them.

"My father doesn't want me dating you. He doesn't think

it will look good for his campaign. He wants everything to look picture-perfect, and..." He helplessly shrugged, looking away briefly. "I guess divorced parents isn't picture-perfect enough for him."

"Are you serious?" She scooted back an inch.

Oh, hell, no. He didn't want her backing away from him. But honestly, he couldn't stop her if she wanted to. If she walked out of his house tonight, it wouldn't be because he wasn't honest. It'd be because he was too honest.

"I told him he could shove his campaign up his ass. Nothing—and nobody—is telling me who to love."

She gasped.

Shit. Too soon?

In for a penny, in for a pound.

"I love you, Chasity. I have for a very long time. I've just had my head stuck up my ass to see it."

"Stu..." Her whispered word died there.

He wanted to shout, *Keep going!* Instead, he answered with a tentative, "Yes?"

She set her beer on the coffee table, then stood up. "I should go."

He sprung to his feet, startling Curley, who popped up to all fours as well on the couch. "Why? Because of my father? Because I said I love you already? Why?"

She shrugged, biting her bottom lip. "I have no idea why. I just think I should leave."

He nodded, feeling a bit of karma biting him in the ass. It was like déjà vu, but the roles reversed. This time, she was doing the leaving, see ya later, it was fun. He deserved it.

He stepped around the coffee table, and nodded again, to confirm to her once more he understood why. She needed time to process it all. He never should've told her what his father said. But he didn't want any lies, any half-truths, any secrets between them. It would've only burned a hole in his chest keeping it to himself.

Curley jumped off the couch and took a spot next to his feet.

Then she walked past him without even a word goodbye. His front door closed with a quiet click.

He sighed.

He swore he heard an audible sigh echo down by his feet.

"She'll be back, right? She'll call? Forgive me?" he asked, looking down. "I was honest. I showed her a part of what my life is like, something I never show anyone. People assume life is good. I act like it is. I showed her what it's really like. She'll be back."

Curley started to wag his tail.

Stu could only take that as a triumphant yes.

15

HER EYES ZONED OUT, staring at the Christmas movie blaring on the TV. She was surprised her neighbor hadn't knocked on her wall it was too loud. The older gentleman living next door never liked it when she watched her shows at a certain volume level. But sometimes, she needed noise. To drown out the chaos going on inside her head.

Well, it was Christmas Eve, so he was likely gone visiting family or something. Good thing, too, because she had no intention of turning down the movie even though she had no clue what was going on.

Her mind couldn't stop drifting away to Stu and the things he told her.

He loved her.

His father thought her family was so terrible she'd make him look bad.

Wow.

Just wow.

She knew Hope talked about the man—even called him a beast—but she had no idea. Sure, she didn't listen to the gossip that made its way around town, but she heard things here and there. After wracking her brain for a tiny memory of one rumor about Mayor Hafferty, she couldn't come up with one. Not one.

Yet, by her sister's account, by his own son's words, he was not a very nice person. How did one get by in town and not be despised on sight? It boggled her mind the more she thought about it.

"Knock, knock."

Her sister's voice trailed her way, then a few seconds later she popped into her view.

"Geez Louise, you have that thing turned up, everyone at Mulberry Diner can hear it."

She chuckled as her sister turned down the volume and plopped down next to her on the couch.

"I tried calling, but you didn't answer." Hope rolled her eyes. "I can see why now. Seriously, what's up with that?"

"I like this movie."

Hope eyed her like she was a suspect waiting in a police lineup. "What's the matter? Something's wrong."

Figures she wouldn't be able to keep anything from her sister. Not when she blatantly acted like this. Seriously, she didn't even know why she was moping. Stu technically hadn't done anything wrong. He had told her the truth of something she wished she didn't know *and* he said he loved her. The last thing should've had her singing from the rooftops, not sulking in self-pity in front of the tv watching a movie she had no idea what was going on.

Chasity offered a sweet grin, then decided to ignore her sister's questioning. She didn't want to talk about it.

"I'm surprised you're not working. The beast not so beastly today?"

Another eye roll punctured her view. That always meant

6

AMANDA SIEGRIST

her sister was in her own sort of mood when she constantly rolled her eyes.

"Don't ignore me. Something's up and I want to know why." She crossed her arms and pursed her lips with a look that said Chasity would not get out of it no matter how much she argued and fought to ignore the issue.

Chasity sighed, then leaned her head against the couch.

"Stu said he loved me last night."

Hope happy squealed, slapping her shoulder playfully. "That's exciting. Why doesn't it seem like this is exciting to you? You were all up in my face about not giving him a chance. What the hell, Chas."

Tilting her head with a pouty lip, she knew what she was about to say would piss off Hope more than it upset her. But one, Hope wasn't going to let it go until she confessed. And two, she had a right to know because she worked for the asshole.

"Do you really want to know?"

"Yes," Hope said as she rolled her eyes once again. "I will disembowel that man with my pinkie nail. Just say the word."

Then she held up her pinkie finger, which indeed had a long ass nail that could cut glass. Of course, the other half of her nails were so short, she wouldn't be surprised if she chewed them like she was gnawing on a piece of black licorice that she loved. Seriously. Who loved black licorice? Only her sister.

Just like that, her dreary mood lifted. She could always count on her sister to make her smile and lift her spirits. Especially with the outrageous things she could say.

After a deep fortifying breath, she told Hope what Stu had told her about Mayor Rafferty. Every last word. It cut as deep as it had last night. Maybe, even more, saying the words herself.

"That bastard," Hope seethed through clenched teeth. Then she exhaled a long breath and laid her head against the couch along with her.

"It doesn't surprise me he would think that. He treats me like dirt most of the time, but not to everyone. I always thought he had a thing against me. Now I know what he truly thinks."

Chasity slid her hand to her sister's and clasped it. "You deserve better. You shouldn't have to deal with any kind of treatment like that."

"I need money to pay the bills."

"Doesn't make it right."

Then they were silent for a moment.

Hope tilted her head in her direction. "So, can I guess if you're sulky like a madwoman, you and Stu didn't end on good terms last night. Like, what's going on with you two?"

"I screwed up. I didn't know what to say. He unloaded so much on me, and I just...I panicked. I left."

Hope sat up, extracting her hands from hers, then combed a few strands of hair behind her ear. "You left? He tells you he loves you and you just...left?"

Chasity sat up as well. "Yeah, and right before that, he told me how horrible his father was."

"Yeah, you big dummie, he also told you he told his father to go suck it."

Giggles erupted between both of them.

Then Hope turned serious. "Look, I know I gave you a hard time about Stu, but what do you want? Do you love him?"

Chasity bit her bottom lip, digging her teeth in, moving them around as she pondered the question. Not that she had to think about it. She knew the answer. It was the question her sister hadn't yet asked that had her in such a quandary.

"Yes, I love him."

"Enough to overlook how much of an asshole his dad is?"

And that was the question that had her confused. Stu already had a rocky relationship with his father. Add her in the mix permanently, and the relationship might totally dissolve. The last thing she wanted to do was be the cause of such a thing. She might not always get along with her dad, but she'd never want to cut him out of her life, and he cut her out of his life. It would break her heart, especially with only one living parent left.

"I'll leave you to your brooding. Hopefully, you have an easy shift so you can really think about it." Hope grabbed the controller and turned the volume back up.

Chasity laughed at how ridiculously loud she turned it up. Of course, it wasn't any louder than what she had it at earlier.

"Where are you going? You could stay for lunch. I don't need to leave for another two hours."

A wicked smile twisted upon Hope's lips. "Oh, I have some things I need to do now."

That made Chasity sit up even straighter. "Like what?"

"Like tell a certain someone where he can shove his dick. Up his own ass."

"You just said you needed that job to pay the bills."

Hope rolled her eyes. "Yeah, but I changed my mind. I can't let it slide. And I also have a great sister who will let me crash on her couch when I can't pay my rent anymore and can't find a job."

"You're so lucky I love you," Chasity shouted as she

threw a decorative pillow that said, "All I want for Christmas is more books" as Hope dashed for the front door. Like she was going to argue about that.

Never. If her sister needed a place to stay, she could stay as long as she liked. More heavy weight from last night shifted off her shoulders that her sister planned to quit. Good. She didn't want her working for that asshole any longer, not after what she learned.

Turning back toward the blaring TV, her mind returned to Stu and the impending doom that she felt awaited her.

Did she love him enough to start a future with him and risk the wrath of his father?

Or did she love him so much she had to let him go so he could live a small semblance of peace and keep a somewhat tentative relationship with his father?

What a complicated answer she didn't have yet.

STU COULDN'T STOP HIMSELF. He paced from one end of the living room to the other. It kind of made him smile when he heard the soft clinking sounds follow him. Curley insisted on pacing with him.

"Sorry, buddy. I'll stop."

Plopping down on the couch, he immediately started to pet Curley under the head for all his hard work walking back and forth. He was supposed to be resting, not walking a mile in a few short steps.

But he couldn't help the nervous energy running through his veins. The day was almost over and no word from Chasity. Not one.

Sure, he understood why she hadn't called this evening

because she was working. But this morning? No call. This afternoon? No call.

Tonight, after her shift...would she call? Come over?

It was Christmas Eve. Not the best day to have a heavy, intense conversation. But it's not like he was celebrating it in the traditional sense. He didn't even visit his mom today like he normally did. Although, he called her about Curley and she understood.

She came over to his house instead. They had lunch. And they had a talk he wished they would've never had.

Of course, she tried to get him to call his father. And say what? That's what he had asked her. Because he wasn't going to push Chasity out of his life. Not for anyone. Especially not for that asshole.

He shouldn't have called his father an asshole in front of his mother. Her eyes had shattered at the word. Not even his Christmas present—a gift certificate to her favorite spa in the Cities—had livened the sparkle in her eyes.

She understood where he was coming from. She had even told his father how wrong he was in what he had asked of him. Yet, she wanted him to be the bigger person and call his father and try to mend their relationship.

No, thanks.

Stu didn't need that kind of negativity in his life.

He shouldn't have said that to his mother either.

She left with sadness in her eyes, her shoulders drooped. While he felt bad about it—and he'd try to call her again tomorrow and apologize for his behavior—he wasn't going to approach his father first. He didn't do anything wrong. His father should say sorry first.

But he never would. He'd never see how wrong he was.

Whatever. Stu knew it was a losing battle.

He only hoped his relationship with Chasity wasn't a losing battle.

Of course, he thought about calling her all day. Making the first move. But he didn't. He didn't have the right. When she was ready to talk, he'd be here waiting.

Curley perked up, his head twisting toward the front hallway when a soft knock sounded on the door.

Stu got excited as well, a bright smile filling his face for the first time that day. Sadly, even his mother hadn't elicited that response from him.

"Do you think she got off early?" Stu glanced at the clock sitting on the fireplace mantel. Eight thirty. Yeah, too hopeful to think she got off that early from work.

He made his way to the door anyway with a hopeful spirit. When he glanced through the peephole and saw the person standing on the other side, he wasn't sure whether to be frightened or not.

He opened the door. Curley sat by his feet.

"Hey, Hope. What a surprise."

"Can I come in or what? It's freezing out." She shivered, whether from the actual brutal temps or to overemphasize how truly cold it was.

He stood to the side—Curley followed as well— and closed the door as soon as she stepped inside.

"So..." he didn't know what to say. Confusion etched across his features at her visit.

Chasity didn't even have any of her belongings at his house, so it's not like she was coming to get them for her.

"Offer me a drink or something? Where are your manners?" she said with a sharp sting of her tongue, yet a sly smirk on her face.

Stu wasn't sure if she was teasing him or not. But with her sudden appearance, he could use a strong drink.

"I got beer, wine, or a bottle of whiskey. Pick your poison," he said as he made his way toward the kitchen.

He heard Curley's click-clack of his nails following him, and Hope's soft steps from her boots. She didn't take them off, but she had the courtesy to wipe her boots on the welcome mat first.

"I'll have whatever you're having."

He looked at her from across the island between them. Then he nodded and pulled two shot glasses down from the cupboard above the stove. Grabbing his whiskey bottle in a separate cupboard near the pantry, he poured two full glasses and pushed one closer to her side.

Picking it up, he gestured her way. "Cheers—whatever we might be cheering."

She dipped her head, then picked up her glass.

They both knocked them back as if they were born to do it. He shivered from the burn as it slid down his throat. She did a full-on body tremble and twisted her lips funny, but she held it down. The woman could take a shot like a pro.

"So..."

He still didn't know what to say.

She set her shot glass down on the island with a wistful smile. "All these years and I never knew you had a thing with my sister. I'm still kind of pissed she kept that from me."

"I'm sorry."

He was. Being the only child, he didn't know what it was like to have a sibling. No sister, no brother. No arguments or petty squabbles about taking up too much bathroom time or not getting out of their room. He had always wanted a sibling, though.

Hope looked at him and nodded. "Your father is the biggest jackass I have ever met."

Chuckling, he nodded this time. "No argument from me. I'm sorry about that, too. Assuming Chasity told you."

"Oh, she told me. Every dirty word." Hope crossed her arms as she pursed her lips. "And I told him what I thought of him."

Damn. He hadn't expected that. Had Chasity confronted him, too? Maybe he should've called her.

"How'd that go?"

"Well, pretty well for me. I didn't give him much chance to speak. But, boy, I feel so much better. I bottled so much inside working for him. I let it all out and then some. Nobody treats my sister like that."

Then she dropped her arms and exhaled loudly. "Although, I am out of a job now. That sucks. But whatever."

"I'm sorry. I wish I knew what to say."

She smiled. Not a condescending or cruel one. More like the wistful one she had before she laid that bomb at his feet.

"I think that's your problem sometimes, Stu. You suck at sharing your feelings. You totally messed up with Chasity."

Yeah, he couldn't disagree there.

"I tried last night."

"I know. You told her you loved her, but you also dropped that other nasty shit on her. Get some common sense, man."

Again. He couldn't disagree, but what was her point?

"Why are you here, Hope? Besides drinking my good whiskey and telling me shit I already know."

"Don't shit on a gifted horse, Stu."

His brows puckered inward, confused. "What? That's not how it goes. It's don't look a gift horse in the mouth."

Hope waved her hand frivolously in the air. "Whatever. You're missing the point here."

He sure was. She was confusing the hell out of him left and right.

"Which is?"

"Do you want my sister back or not?"

He stood up straighter. He swore he heard Curley shift next to him as well, as if ready to hear more.

"Hell, yes."

"Okay, then. You gotta do everything I say and she'll be putty in your hands."

Wow. A Christmas miracle. Delivered right to his doorstep. He couldn't wait to hear every single word she had to say.

"GIVE YOUR OLD GRANDPA A HUG."

Chasity smiled as she leaned in and hugged her grandpa. The day had been going well so far. And it was Christmas, so it should. She had a few bad Christmas memories, especially the year her parents got divorced, and since then, she had sworn she'd have a good Christmas every year. Because nobody should be sad around Christmastime.

She had a nice lunch with her grandpa, Hope, and a few other residents from the retirement home. A delicious feast that would keep her stuffed well into the night. Hopefully, Hope wasn't making anything too serious for supper tonight. Before they left, she would mention to her not to make anything heavy. She didn't think she'd have room for much. She had already made butter horns this morning. Their dessert. She had even brought a plate full to the retirement home for everyone. They had been a huge hit. She couldn't wait to stuff her face with more tonight.

She hugged her grandpa a little tighter.

"What's the matter, pumpernickel?" He leaned away but

didn't let go of her. "You've been..." He paused as if looking for the right word. "...far away this afternoon."

"I have a lot on my mind."

Her grandpa patted the couch near them and they both sat down.

"Unload on me. I can give you some wise insight."

Chasity chuckled, already feeling marginally better. Her grandpa could always manage to brighten her mood with few words. Usually, his presence calmed her, centered her equilibrium.

"Is our family dysfunctional? Like, cringeworthy dysfunctional?"

"Aren't all families dysfunctional in their own way? Nobody is perfect. Therefore, no family is perfect. My grand-po-meter says this might have something to do with Stu and his father."

"Ding, ding, ding," she said because his meter hit the mark.

"I know Stu is a good man, but his father can be—" Her grandpa shook his head back and forth, looking for another good word to use. "A jackass."

She burst out laughing, her mood lifting even more. Leave it to her grandpa to say it like it is.

Her grandpa reached out and cupped her hand lying on her knee. "Look, any decision you make will be the right one. We should never regret anything in life. I'm an old man. I've made many mistakes, but I don't regret anything. Those mistakes I made, made me into who I am. They molded my life into the way it was meant to be. So, you take whatever is weighing on you, and you ask yourself, will I regret this?"

"Thanks, Grandpa. I always appreciate your wisdom."

He patted her hand. "You're welcome, pumpernickel.

Now go swipe two more butter horns for us before that plate completely empties."

She laughed as she stood up. Heading to the table, she grabbed three butter horns, giving her grandpa two of them. He winked in thanks.

She and Hope left about an hour later after playing a game of cards with their grandpa and Chuck. Hope promised not to make a heavy meal, and they agreed Chasity would come by around six. That gave her a few hours on her own to figure out how to proceed with Stu.

She should call him. At least wish him a merry Christmas. Although, he hadn't reached out to her either, so maybe she shouldn't.

Of course, he could be waiting for her to make the first move.

Ugh.

She was so confused about how to proceed.

Well, she didn't want to have a bad Christmas, so she made the executive decision to call him tomorrow. Therefore, she wouldn't risk any potential arguments between them. Not that she wanted to argue with him. That was the last thing she wanted.

All she wanted for Christmas this year was to confess she loved him back and not worry about their future.

That wasn't going to happen.

She got bored waiting to head to her sister's, so she took a bath, considering Hope told her she couldn't come over early.

Why not? It had been so odd, and she had even suggested they binge-watch a bunch of Christmas classics.

But Hope wouldn't budge, saying she had some things she needed to do. On Christmas? What could she need to do on Christmas? Not wanting to argue with her sister, she accepted it. Sometimes—ha! Most times—her sister was very bullheaded about things and it was useless to argue with her.

Her bath was relaxing, and honestly, what she needed. She didn't realize it until she was soaking in the hot water, a small pool of bubbles floating around. She tried to read, but the words blurred together. Her mind was so unfocused, she laid there with her head against the wall, her eyes closed, enjoying the soothing heat.

When the water started to get cold, she figured she had relaxed long enough. By the time she got out, redressed, and fixed her hair, it was only about twenty minutes until she could head for her sister's.

She grabbed the container full of butter horns, a bottle of white wine, and decided if she showed up a few minutes early, it wouldn't be that bad. Hope would have to get over it.

Heading out into the brutal cold, she dashed for her car and turned the heater on, rubbing her gloved hands near the vent.

It didn't take long to make it to her sister's. Grabbing the container and bottle of wine, she stepped out of her car and walked carefully to her sister's house she rented. With all the snow they had gotten off and on the past week, her sidewalk was a bit slippery. She saw some sand tossed here and there, but not enough to help. She'd have to holler at her sister for her shoddy job at sanding down her sidewalk.

Light, fresh snowflakes suddenly appeared, dropping onto her face. Looking up, she smiled at the pretty sight. Snow could be a real pain in the ass, especially during Minnesota winters, but she always enjoyed snow on Christmas. The pretty snowflakes fell peacefully, touching her nose, her cheeks, her white fluffy hat on her head.

A perfect way to end a good day. With some snow.

Walking up the few steps to the porch, she used the bottom of the wine bottle to hit the doorbell. Normally, she'd simply walk in, but her hands were full and the porch was almost worse than the sidewalk. She almost slipped when she stepped onto the porch. It would've made her cry, not only from hurting her butt from the fall, but it would've most likely broken the wine bottle. And she wanted a glass of wine as soon as her sister let her in. That would've rounded out her bath perfectly, except she hadn't wanted to drink and drive. She had every intention of spending the night at her sister's.

The door swung open.

Stu stood in front of her.

The wine bottle slipped from her hand.

HE WAS NEVER one for sports, something his father hadn't been too disappointed in. He had much rather Stu focus on his studies and get impeccable grades. Sports would've only hindered that.

But he was thankful for quick reflexes when Chasity dropped the wine bottle. He reached out and caught it before it hit the porch.

"Oh, shit. Good catch," she said with a chuckle. Then her brows puckered. "What are you doing here?"

He let out a slow breath, praying Hope hadn't steered him wrong. Chasity didn't look happy to see him.

"Cooking supper...and hoping we can have a good night together."

"But...but..." Chasity's frown intensified. "With my sister? Where is she?"

Then Chasity stepped inside, swiping past him with

determination in her gaze. He shut the door and watched as she jaunted up the stairs, shouting for her sister.

So far, not going as well as Hope said it would. But he wasn't going to let it deter him. He'd see it all through.

Heading toward the kitchen, figuring Chasity would see Hope wasn't here and seek him out. He didn't want the food to burn. Hope had said Chasity didn't want a heavy meal, which had made him scramble and rethink his entire meal plan. He'd had every intention of making a nice honey glazed ham with mashed potatoes and freshly made bread. It was Christmas, after all.

After Hope's warning, he opted to make a wild rice hot dish that his mother made to perfection every single time. He had never attempted it, so he called his mother for some tips. He heard the sadness in her voice that he hadn't reached out to his father yet, but he also heard the glee emerge when he said why he wanted to make the hot dish. Because he was trying to woo Chasity.

Checking the dish, the wild rice looking cooked and done, the dish itself bubbling and smelling delicious, he decided it was time to take it out. Grabbing two potholders, he removed the dish from the oven and set it on the counter, inhaling.

Damn. That smelled like heaven. He couldn't wait to dive in and eat an entire plateful. Hopefully, it wasn't too heavy for Chasity. Unlike her, he hadn't had much for lunch. Curley had a nice special wet dog food since it was Christmas, and he had a turkey sandwich with a bag of chips. Nothing very special about that.

"Wow, that smells delicious."

He jumped, turning around to see Chasity standing in the doorway. "Wild rice hot dish. My mom's specialty. I hope I didn't screw it up."

Her eyes lit up with delight. "With the way it smells, I doubt it." Then she frowned. "Where's my sister?"

He took a step toward her. This was the moment. She'd either forgive him—or at least understand he didn't have the same views as his father—and enjoy the evening with him. Or she'd leave, not wanting anything to do with him.

"She's hanging out with Curley."

Chasity bit her bottom lip. "This was all her idea, wasn't it?"

"To let me have the night with you? Yes. I picked the meal. I'm very grateful she doesn't hate me. I—"

"I don't hate you, Stu," Chasity said, cutting him off, taking a step toward him.

His heart started to pound. With a bit of anticipation she was on the verge of falling into his arms *and* with a bit of apprehension she would slap him in the face.

It could honestly go either way.

"But you're not happy with me either. I'm sorry. I truly am. I refuse to let my father ruin my life in any way, and that includes pushing you away. I should've never pushed you away all those years ago. I regret it so much." He took another step closer, even with the potential rejection on the horizon.

She closed the distance, brushing her hand across his cheek.

"We should never regret anything. And I know I'll regret it if I don't tell you I love you, too."

"Really?" he asked in a whisper as he placed his hands on her waist. "Because I love you so damn much. I had a miserable day yesterday, missing you. Thinking about you. Wanting to talk to you."

"I'm sorry I walked out. You unloaded a lot on me and I just…" She shrugged. "Panicked. But I love you. I want you.

But I don't want to be the cause of any more rift between you and your dad."

"He'll never change. I'm not waiting for him to accept anything about my life." Then he pressed his lips to hers, pulling her closer.

She melted into his embrace, kissing him back. Her hands wove up his back and through his hair as the kiss deepened. A low throaty moan escaped, and he knew he wouldn't be able to wait long before he'd need to be even closer to her. Deep, deep inside her.

Supper could wait.

Lifting her up, she giggled against his lips as she wrapped her legs around his waist.

"Where are you taking me?"

"To our makeshift hotel room for the night."

He walked the short distance to the living room where Hope had helped him blow up an air mattress and fill it with blankets and pillows galore. She said the house could get drafty, so lots of blankets were necessary. He intended to use body heat to keep warm all night long. Chasity wouldn't be far from his side if he had anything to say about it.

"So, we're spending the night here, are we?" Beautiful laughter fell from her lips when he tossed her onto the mountain of blankets, covering her body with his.

"Oh, yeah. All night long. Just you and me. I have supper done. I have a nice bottle of white wine—along with yours —and a few Christmas movies we can watch together. Because I know you love those sappy Christmas movies." He leaned back and pointed toward the coffee table pushed to the side near the wall where he had a computer set up. "Oh, and it wouldn't be a festive night without a roaring fire."

Chasity followed his finger to see a video of a fire playing on the screen.

"My hero. You put out all the stops for me. So romantic."

He kissed her, her eyes finally lit up with happiness with her lips twisted into a gorgeous smile.

"I love you. I will show you every single day just how much if you let me."

She sighed happily as her fingers trailed up his back and through his hair again. "I love you, too. I do believe I will let you. No regrets."

"Never having regrets again in my life."

Then he sealed the deal with a kiss.

Merry, merry Christmas to him. She was the only present he needed.

EPILOGUE

Three days later

THE COLD BITE of the wind wasn't going to deter her. Not one bit. Nor the devilish look twisted on his lips. She was in it to win it.

But the wind was very brutal today. And the trek up Dragon Hill was always a beast. Even though this was only her second time climbing it, she was going with *always*. Her thigh muscles were killing her and they were only halfway up.

She had to focus her mind on something else, and she was a bit curious why Stu hadn't said anything to her yet about how his lunch went.

"So..."

Stu grinned at her, looking like he was barely breaking a sweat. He wore aviator sunglasses today, and it bummed her out because she couldn't read his eyes. Although the mischievous smile still plastered on his face told her enough.

"So..." he copied, cocking a brow.

"You had lunch today with Elliot."

His smile dipped. "Wow, news travels fast. I was going to tell you about it. I just didn't want to ruin the mood."

She bent down and threw a small handful of snow at him. She giggled at the way he dodged yet didn't move fast enough as some hit his cheek.

"I won't let anything ruin my mood."

He nodded with a smirk. "You're going to pay for that later."

Oh, she couldn't wait to see how he dished out his payback. Hopefully with dirty kisses and his tender touch in unseen places.

"So, yeah, I had lunch with Elliot and my dad showed up. We had a chat. He shockingly apologized for what he said about you and what he asked me to do."

Chasity stopped. One, because that surprised the hell out of her, too. Sure, he had reached out to Hope to get her to take her job back—which she still refused to do—but he hadn't apologized to Hope in any way. Two, because she needed a small breather. The exertion up the hill this time was a little harder. Maybe from the colder temperature and the wind was a bit stronger today.

"Really?"

"Yeah, weird, right?" Stu chuckled. "Don't worry, he had assholery moments. He still wants me to drop the bar and follow in his footsteps. Help with his campaign. I told him I'd put one of his signs in the parking lot and that was about the extent of my help I'd offer."

"Well, I'm glad to hear it went fairly well."

They started to climb once more.

"Me, too. I don't like being at odds with my dad, but he makes it so easy most of the time."

She brought up the conversation, and suddenly felt bad

she might've ruined his mood. So, she bent down and scooped up another small batch of snow and tossed it his way.

This time he had no idea it was coming and it hit the side of his face.

"Oh, you are so going to pay for that," he said with a sly smile.

Then he darted in her direction. But she anticipated him doing something of the sort and she picked up her pace. They raced up the hill, laughter and giggles permeating the air.

When she reached the top, she was completely out of breath and couldn't move another muscle. Stu tossed the sled to the side and brought her to the ground with a playful shove. She landed in the soft snow with him above her.

His warm lips caressed hers.

She would never get sick of these moments.

Since Christmas, they had been inseparable. After a fun-filled night at her sister's, cuddling in front of the fake fire, watching Christmas movies, and eating that delicious hot dish, she knew she made the right decision. Life was merrier with Stu by her side.

"So..." he murmured against her lips. "Loser does the dishes for a week...naked."

She belted out laughing. Of course, he'd twist it into something sensual. She couldn't wait to see him standing in front of the sink doing the dishes—naked.

"Deal."

Then they sealed it with a searing, scorching kiss that warmed her body like she was laying in front of a crackling fire.

Stu slowed the kiss down and rolled until he was lying

next to her in the snow. "That walk up the hill is always brutal."

"Right." Glad she wasn't the only one who thought that.

A bright smile filtered onto her face as a tiny snowflake landed on her cheek. Then another. And another.

"It's snowing."

Up here, lying in the snow, looking up at the bright blue sky with gentle snowflakes falling around, it didn't faze her. It was a beautiful sight.

She hoped it stopped later, though, as she was sick of driving in it.

Stu grabbed her hand. She turned her head and met his whiskey-colored gaze.

"Ready to lose? Because I can't wait to see you naked."

She winked. "You're on. Let's do it."

They stood up and brushed off, then positioned the sled.

Stu sat down first and pointed behind him. "Do over from the last time. You can sit behind me again."

"I'm not falling off this time. I will be winning."

She scooted on behind him, wrapping her arms around his waist.

"Hold on, sweetheart. It's gonna be brutal."

That was no lie.

The sharp wind on her face.

The cold temperatures.

The need to win.

She couldn't wait.

Holding Stu tightly, she signaled she was ready and off they went, flying down the hill, snow pelting their face.

What a ride. Full of fun and laughter, and silly, silly bets.

Best Christmas present she would've never thought to ask for.

Stu by her side. Always.

———

DON'T MISS THE NEXT BOOK IN THIS HEARTWARMING HOLIDAY
SERIES!
HOLIDAY HOPE

A QUICK NOTE...

I hope you enjoyed Stu & Chasity's story! Curley, the dog in the story, was inspired by my dog I had! His name was Curley! He passed away two years ago, and it still hurts when I think about him. I miss him so much! Best dog ever! I didn't have any intention to add him in the story. It just happened. His mannerisms, like following Stu all around the house were true, like my Curley. He followed me everywhere. I left the room, so did he. He slept by me at night, even under the covers. He loved to snuggle. When I say he was my fur baby, he totally was. I got him from the SPCA in Baltimore. He had been found wandering the streets, dirty, knotted hair, and malnourished. I'm so glad I had the chance to be his mom and give him a loving home. I want to dedicate this book to all those fur babies out there that we love and cherish.

♥ MUCH LOVE,
AMANDA SIEGRIST

FOR ELLIOT & LYNN'S STORY
MERRY ME
A HOLIDAY ROMANCE NOVEL, #1

He never knew a simple gift left on his porch step would mend his wounded heart.

Hiding his dislike for the holidays isn't easy, especially when Chief Elliot Duncan meets a woman who captures his attention with one sweet smile. Lynn Carpenter is beautiful, strong-willed, and hardworking, and he doesn't know how to return her gift that was left on his porch by mistake. As Christmas approaches, it doesn't take much for the holiday spirit to seep in, not when Lynn makes it so effortless with her excitement. The only thing he wants for Christmas this year is her heart. But between his meddling father and the need to take care of her, something she passionately resists, he knows it won't be that simple. He's up for the challenge, because losing Lynn is unacceptable.

FOR AIDEN & THERESA'S STORY
MISTLETOE MAGIC
A HOLIDAY ROMANCE NOVEL, #2

A mistletoe. A kiss. This just might be the start of a beautiful Christmas.

Theresa might not make the best pot of coffee in town, but people still flock to the diner for a cup, even Officer Crowl, who rarely displays a smile since his fiancé died. She'll never be able to win his heart, but it's hard to resist him, especially when he kisses her under the mistletoe. Well, on the cheek, but that has to count for something...right?

Staying busy keeps Officer Aiden Crowl sane. Because when he's idle or alone, he thinks, and nothing good comes from that. Everyone thinks he's the perfect man. They think he's broken because she's gone. He is, just not for the reason they believe. Every time he walks into the diner, one sweet smile from Theresa erases some of the pain. He should stay away from her. Far away. But what is he supposed to do when they're standing under a mistletoe? Kiss her, of course.

FOR BENTLEY & EMMA'S STORY
CHRISTMAS WISH
A HOLIDAY ROMANCE NOVEL, #3

What if you had one wish granted for Christmas? What would it be?

Acting reckless isn't something Bentley Wilson is known for, but when he runs back into a burning building to save a little girl's puppy after specifically told not to do so, that's exactly how most of the town sees him, especially the fire chief who insists he has to help with the annual Christmas party because of his behavior. Throw in the fact the woman he's pined over for too long is getting married, this holiday is going to go down as one of the worst. Until he meets Emma Brookes. She's feisty, headstrong, and holds so much pain hidden in the depths of her beautiful green eyes. He wants nothing more than to erase her sadness. But it's already a season of disaster, and every time they're together, they spar like two warriors dueling to the death. Despite that, he likes the challenge, the crazy way she makes him feel. Before the holiday is over, he vows to get his one Christmas wish. That she never leaves his side.

FOR JAMES & ERIN'S STORY
SNOWED IN LOVE
A HOLIDAY ROMANCE NOVEL, #4

A blizzard. A cabin. A cup of hot chocolate.
The perfect mixture to fall in love.

James Brennen is nothing but a screwup. At least, in the small town of Mulberry, that's what everyone thinks of him. As a recovering alcoholic, he's trying his best to turn his life around, to be a better man. All of his hard work comes crashing down when he's fired from his job at the hospital—accused of stealing drugs. Nothing ever changes and he's done trying to prove himself. Needing time alone, his friend's cabin in the middle of the woods provides the perfect escape. He knows he's found deep trouble, not only when he gets stranded during a brutal snowstorm, but that he's stuck with the one woman he's wanted since the first day he laid eyes on her. The passion burns bright between them, but it doesn't matter, because as soon as Christmas is over, he's leaving for good.

For Mase & Hope's Story
Holiday Hope
A Holiday Romance Novel, #6

Let the merriment begin...Operation Holiday Hope commence.

Life hasn't been the same since she quit her job working for the tyrant mayor, but Hope Bronson is trying her best. She's attempting to embrace the holiday spirit and pretend she's happy when, in reality, she feels stuck in a rut. And why? She can't even explain it to herself, let alone to anyone else, without risking being called a drama queen. And men... don't even get her started. Talk about bad choices every. Single. Time. Except...maybe one guy, but she can't trust her own judgment. It doesn't matter that everyone tells her he's a good one. She's leery of opening herself up to another bad decision—unless he can convince her otherwise.

Mase Brandt can't believe his luck when he's asked to fix a Nativity scene for the church. The one and only woman to steal his heart with ease works there. A few months ago, she shut him out with little fanfare. This time, he's not giving up so easily. The holidays are a joyous time of year. He'll use anything and everything to his advantage to win her heart. He knows she won't make a moment of it easy on him. But that's okay. He has a few tricks up his sleeve. Let the festivities begin.

FOR CAM & SERENITY'S STORY
SLEIGH ALL THE WAY
A HOLIDAY ROMANCE NOVEL, #7

There's no such thing as too much holiday cheer...right?

If there's one thing Cam is good at, it's working with his hands. So making a sleigh for the woman who loves Christmas with a passion seems like a foolproof plan to win her heart. He's done being stuck in the friend zone. Except he's a little rusty with dating. After keeping women at a distance for so long, he's going to need more help than he realized. Who knew he'd get it from where he least expected it—her twin boys. This should be easy-peasy. But one thing Cam has learned: nothing ever works out like he plans.

Serenity doesn't like it known, but she hates Christmas. With a passion. The last thing she can do is let anyone know, especially her boys. She'd never ruin the holiday for them. Besides faking holiday cheer, she finds herself having to resist the one man who is impossible to resist. Cam is everything she always wanted in a guy: kind, caring, always there for her when she needs him. But they're friends, and losing him from her life can't happen. Venturing into the sex-zone would ruin it all. If there is one thing she's good at, it's pretending. All she has to do is make him believe being friends is for the best.

ABOUT THE AUTHOR

I'm a *USA Today* Bestselling Author that loves to write contemporary romance and romantic suspense novels, although I am partial to romantic suspense. I even dabble in paranormal. Honestly, I love anything that has to do with romance. As long as there's a happy ending, I'm a happy camper. And insta-love...yes, please! I love baseball (Go Twins!) and creating awesome crafts. I graduated with a Bachelor's Degree in Criminal Justice, working in that field for several years before I became a stay-at-home mom. I have a few more amazing stories in the works. If you would like to learn more about me and my books, head to my website by scanning the QR code. Thanks for reading!

Scan me

www.ingramcontent.com/pod-product-compliance
Lightning Source LLC
Chambersburg PA
CBHW030330030726
47499CB00003B/719